Varjak Paw

SF Said

Illustrated by
Dave McKean

dfb

David Fickling Books

OXFORD · NEW YORK

31 Beaumont Street
Oxford OX1 2NP, UK

VARJAK PAW
A DAVID FICKLING BOOK 978 1 849 92057 5

First published in Great Britain by David Fickling Books,
a division of Random House Children's Books
A Random House Group Company

Hardback edition published 2003
Corgi edition published 2004
This edition published 2010

5 7 9 10 8 6

The Random House Group Limited supports The Forest Stewardship Council (FSC®), the
leading international forest certification organisation. Our books carrying the FSC label are
printed on FSC® certified paper. FSC is the only forest certification scheme endorsed by
the leading environmental organisations, including Greenpeace. Our paper procurement
policy can be found at www.randomhouse.co.uk/environment

MIX
Paper from
responsible sources
FSC
www.fsc.org   FSC® C016897

Set in 12/15pt New Baskerville

DAVID FICKLING BOOKS
31 Beaumont Street, Oxford, OX1 2NP

www.**kids**at**random**house.co.uk

Addresses for companies within The Random House Group Limited
can be found at: www.randomhouse.co.uk/offices.htm

THE RANDOM HOUSE GROUP Limited Reg. No. 954009

A CIP catalogue record for this book is available from the British Library.

Printed and bound by CPI Group (UK) Ltd, Croydon, CR0 4YY

'There's no place like home.'

The Wizard of Oz

Chapter One

The Elder Paw was telling a story.

It was a Jalal tale, one of the best. Varjak loved to hear his grandfather's tales of their famous ancestor: how Jalal fought the fiercest warrior cats, how he was the mightiest hunter, how he came out of Mesopotamia and travelled to the ends of the earth, further than any cat had been before.

But today, the Elder Paw's tale just made Varjak restless. So what if Jalal had such exciting adventures? Varjak never would. Jalal had ended his days in the Contessa's house. His family of Mesopotamian Blues had stayed here ever since.

The old place must have been full of light and life in Jalal's time, generations ago – but now it was full of dust and musty smells. The windows were always closed, the doors locked. There was a garden, but it was surrounded by a high stone wall. Jalal was the last to cross it. In all the years since then, no one had ever left the Contessa's house.

Now, no one except Varjak was even listening to the tale of Jalal's adventures. Father, Mother and Aunt Juni were dozing in the late afternoon light that trickled through the thick green windows. His big brother Julius was flexing his muscles; his cousin Jasmine was fiddling with her collar. His litter brothers Jay, Jethro and Jerome were playing one of those kittenish games that Varjak could never see the point of, and wasn't allowed to join in anyway.

No one was looking at him. This was his chance. He'd been in the garden before, but the family didn't like it out there, and never let him stay very long.

Stealthy as Jalal himself, Varjak rose up and padded to the cat door. He could see the garden on the other side. He could almost feel the fresh air, brushing through his whiskers. He nudged it open –

'Varjak Paw!' It was Father. 'Where do you think you're going?'

Varjak spun around. The tale was over; they'd woken up and seen him. But this time, he wouldn't give in.

'Aren't we allowed in the garden, now?' he said.

'Sweetheart,' said Mother, coming over and straightening his collar, 'the garden is a nasty, dirty place. You're a pedigree cat. A pure-bred Mesopotamian Blue. What do you want out there?'

Varjak looked around: at the stuffy furniture, the locked-up cupboards, the curtains he wasn't allowed to climb. He'd never been anywhere else, but this had to be the most boring place on earth.

'Hunting,' he said. 'Aren't we supposed to hunt? The tales talk about—'

'Tales!' snorted his big brother Julius, green eyes glinting. It was said that their ancestor Jalal had green eyes. Everyone in the family had them – everyone but Varjak Paw. 'Tales are for kittens,' scoffed Julius. Cousin Jasmine giggled; Varjak bristled.

'Jalal was a long, long time ago,' said Mother, smoothing and grooming Varjak's silver-blue fur, until he wriggled away. 'Anyway, Jalal came to live in the Contessa's house for a good reason. The tales also say there are monsters Outside, huge monsters called dogs, so fierce that even people fear them.' She shuddered. 'No, we're lucky that the Contessa loves us, and lets us live here.'

'The Contessa loves *some* of us,' interrupted Julius. Varjak knew what was coming; and worse, he thought it might be true. 'When I was a kitten,' boasted Julius, 'the Contessa was down here every day. She used to let me play on her lap, she made a fuss of me. But now she only ever comes down to feed us, and sometimes she doesn't even do that. In fact, we've hardly seen her at all – since that funny-looking Varjak was born.'

Cousin Jasmine giggled again. This time, Varjak's litter brothers Jay, Jethro and Jerome joined in.

'It's because of his eyes,' added Julius. 'The colour of danger. A Mesopotamian Blue whose eyes aren't green – it's an embarrassment.'

That did it. Julius was bigger than him, and older, but Varjak couldn't help it. He faced up to Julius, fur rising with anger.

'I don't believe you,' he said. 'You're a liar.'

'Varjak!' said Father. 'That's no way to talk to your brother!'

'But Julius said—'

'Whine, whine, whine,' sneered Julius. 'Listen to the little insect whine.'

'Julius, you shouldn't tease him so much,' said Father. 'The Contessa's upstairs because she's ill, nothing more. But Varjak Paw – you have to learn to behave like a proper Mesopotamian Blue. We're noble cats, special cats. We don't run around calling each other liars. We don't talk about disgusting things like hunting. And we don't get our paws all muddy in the garden. That's *not* what being a Blue is about. Do you understand?'

Varjak's tail curled up. It was always like this. Julius could get away with anything; but everything Varjak did was wrong.

'Your father's talking to you,' said Aunt Juni sternly. 'Do you understand?'

He stared down at the cold stone floor, silent. There was nothing he could say.

'Fine,' said Father. 'Suit yourself. But until you learn to act like a Blue, there'll be no supper for you.' He licked his chops. 'Come on, everyone. Let's eat.'

They all headed down the corridor to the kitchen, leaving Varjak on his own in the hallway between the stairs and front door. Last to go was the Elder Paw, the head of the family.

'Don't worry, Varjak,' he whispered, so no one else could hear. 'I'll tell you another Jalal tale tonight – one about his greatest battle.' He winked, and then joined the rest of them.

It made things a little better. Even if the tales made Varjak restless, he loved them. They were the closest he'd ever get to adventure in this place. He looked at the old, wooden stairs, covered in dusty carpet. The cats weren't allowed up there now the Contessa was ill. Her door was always shut.

The whole house was like that. No one came in and no one went out. Nothing new or exciting ever happened. It was the dullest life a cat could have.

creeaak

The front door swung open. A blast of wind swirled in, sweeping all the dust into the air. Varjak's fur stood on end.

click CLACK

Two shiny black shoes. Each big as a cat. Coming through the door.

Heart racing, Varjak bent back his head, to follow the line above the shoes. Up a pair of legs, up some more, he saw huge white hands, huge enough to hold his whole body, strong enough to break his neck.

He had to crane back even further, till it hurt, to see the face. It was a man Varjak had never seen before. It was hard to make out the man's eyes for the shadows of his brow, but his full pink lips glistened wetly in the half-light.

The lips creased and opened, and out came a voice that rumbled like thunder, far above Varjak's head. The man strode into the hallway.

Varjak felt dizzy. He looked down. By the man's shiny black shoes, there were two sleek black cats, stalking into the Contessa's house. They were nothing like Mesopotamian Blues. They looked much larger and stronger, even than Father or Julius, and there was something frightening about the way they moved. As if they were two parts of one body, working together perfectly. Too perfect. Varjak glanced from one to the other, and couldn't tell them apart.

They came right up to him, and looked down at him with identical eyes; eyes as smooth and black as their fur. He trembled.

'Who are you?' he said. There was no flicker of understanding in their eyes, no expression: nothing. They just pushed him aside as if he wasn't even there, and took up positions, flanking the staircase.

And now other men came into the house. Their shiny black shoes clicked past Varjak, one by one by one. It was all he could see of them. Frozen to the spot, mind spinning, he watched these giants pass

14

the black cats, climb the stairs – and enter the room
where the Blues weren't allowed to go.

Chapter Two

What should he do? Things like this just didn't happen in the Contessa's house.

Tell the family. They'd know what to do.

Varjak rushed down the corridor. He could feel two pairs of identical black eyes watching him – but the cats didn't follow. They stayed by the stairs, guarding the way up.

Fear and confusion scorched through Varjak's veins as he turned the corner. He raced to the kitchen, fast as he could go, faster still. Who were these cats? Who were the men? What did they want?

He skidded to a halt by the kitchen; hesitated by the doorway. Everything seemed so normal. The whole family was in there. They were eating supper, munching and crunching from rows of china bowls, neat and regular: bowls of food, bowls of water, round white saucers of full-cream milk.

He felt like a stranger, watching from a distance. They looked so grand, with their perfectly groomed silver-blue fur, their green eyes, their tidy little collars around their necks.

'So, you're ready to behave like a proper Blue,' said Father. 'Very good.'

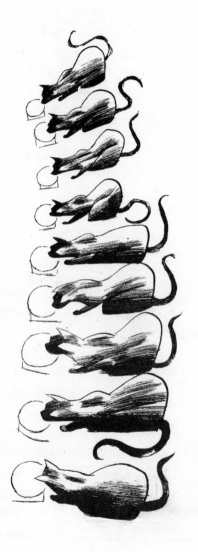

'Have you washed your paws?' said Mother.

'There are cats!' shouted Varjak. 'There are black cats in the house, and they—'

'Varjak . . .' said Mother.

'– they came with a man –'

'Varjak!' said Father.

'He's gone up to the Contessa's room!'

There was silence in the kitchen. The munching and crunching stopped. They all watched him: one great, green, accusing eye.

'I just don't understand him,' muttered Father. 'Why can't he be like everyone else?'

'You haven't washed your paws, have you sweetheart?' said Mother. She came over and started scrubbing.

Varjak bit his tongue. No one believed a word he said. It wasn't fair. In the middle of his family he felt friendless and alone.

'Come and eat with us, Varjak,' said cousin Jasmine. 'The food's ever so nice.' Jasmine's voice was cool and smooth, like milk in the morning.

'I don't want to eat,' he tried to explain. 'There are black cats in the house—'

'Oh, who cares what that little insect does?' said Julius. '*I'll* have Varjak's food. You have to eat to build your muscles.' Julius puffed himself up, and tucked into Varjak's bowl. Jasmine looked impressed.

'You hear that, Varjak?' said Father proudly.

'Julius is a proper Mesopotamian Blue.'

Varjak bristled. Julius might be the family hero, but Varjak knew something no one else did, something important. How could he make them believe him?

'On Jalal's name, I swear it's true,' he insisted. 'The cats are guarding the stairs right now. I looked into their eyes.' He shivered at the memory. 'They're all black.'

'Enough!' yelled Father. 'That's enough of these – these tales!' He spat out the word 'tales' with particular disgust.

'Ah, but some tales are true,' said the Elder Paw quietly. 'Why don't you show us, Varjak? Take us to the cats.'

Father scowled at the Elder Paw, but kept quiet. The head of the family always had final say. Varjak's grandfather was getting old – his fine fur was almost all silver – and he seldom spoke up these days; but everyone listened when he did.

Stomach knotted with nerves, Varjak led them down the corridor. He turned the corner into the hallway, just in time to glimpse a blur of movement by the front door. The first man was holding it open for the others. They were carrying something away. Down by their shoes, two black tails swished out of the house.

The man shut the door as the rest of Varjak's family

entered the hallway. They hadn't seen the others, or the black cats. All they could see was the man.

'Why, it's a Gentleman,' said Mother.

'I remember when we were kittens,' said Aunt Juni, 'there were Ladies and Gentlemen here every day. The Contessa always had visitors.'

They looked up the stairs. The Contessa's door was wide open. There was no one in her room. It was empty.

Surprise rippled around the family. Not knowing what to think, they peered up at the Gentleman – all except the Elder Paw, who seemed thoughtful, as if he was trying to remember something.

The Gentleman pointed up at the Contessa's room, and said something in his voice like thunder, high above their heads. Then he crouched down, bringing himself closer to their level. His wet pink lips smiled at each of them in turn.

Varjak glanced nervously at the front door. The black cats hadn't come back. He hoped they wouldn't.

With a flourish, the Gentleman brought something out of his pocket. He held it out on his waxy white hand, and murmured to the family. Curious, they edged a little closer, to see what it was.

A toy mouse.

Small, grey, furry: it was perfect in every way, so precisely detailed it could almost be alive.

The Gentleman placed it on the floor in front of

them. Varjak sniffed the mouse. It even smelled real. A tingle of wonder ran through him. He'd always wanted to hunt a mouse.

'Let me see that,' said Father. He examined the toy. 'Amazing,' he purred, and batted it across to Julius. Julius flipped it stylishly, through the air, to Jay, to Jethro, to Jerome. They giggled. Varjak wondered if he'd get it back. Probably not.

'What a beautiful toy,' said Mother.

'It's the best present we've ever had,' cooed Jasmine.

The Gentleman smiled, and stood up to his full height. He waved at them to follow, as his shiny black shoes went clicking towards the kitchen. Jay, Jethro and Jerome raced to be first beside him.

'Come on,' said Father. 'Let's see what he's going to do next.'

In the kitchen, the Gentleman was spooning something into their bowls. It was an oily black paste, with a sharp fishy smell. Varjak's nose wrinkled at it.

'Ugh!' he said.

'That's caviare,' whispered Mother. 'The rarest, most expensive food in the world.'

'Treats like this are only given to the finest pedigree cats,' purred Father. 'The Gentleman knows how important we are.'

The man put the bowls back on the floor, heaped high with fishy food, and beamed down at them. His pink lips glistened as the cats started to sniff the caviare. He nodded, turned and left the kitchen, smiling all the way.

'What was all the fuss about, Varjak?' said Father, the moment he was gone. 'And that black cat nonsense—'

'I'm calling a Family Council,' interrupted the

Elder Paw. '*Now*. Everyone is to attend, even the kittens.'

'But Elder Paw,' protested Father, eyeing the bowls of caviare. 'Family Council is only for emergencies. It's—'

'Now,' repeated the Elder Paw. 'Now, in the front room.'

The Elder Paw strode away. Varjak glanced anxiously at Father's face. It was twisted with speechless rage.

Chapter Three

'Family Council is now in session,' declared the Elder Paw above the hubbub in the front room.

Mother, Father and Aunt Juni were whispering to one another, huddled together on a rug so old it had lost its pattern and faded away. Julius and Jasmine were sitting behind them, nodding seriously, as if they were grown-ups too. Jay, Jethro and Jerome were fighting over the toy mouse, trying to push each other into the flames of the antique fireplace.

At the Elder Paw's words, they all settled down. Varjak was sitting quietly, on his own at the back, but his mind was burning. This was his first Family Council.

From the Contessa's red velvet armchair, where he stood, the Elder Paw began to speak. 'The family tales tell us that when our ancestor Jalal came out of Mesopotamia, he wandered the earth for many years, before finding a home with the Contessa. Generations of Paws have lived in this house since Jalal's time. But those days may be coming to an end. I believe the Contessa is dead.'

The older cats gasped. They shot strange looks at one another, and shook their heads. A log crackled loudly in the fireplace.

The Elder Paw waited until it was quiet again to continue. 'She has seldom left her room of late, only to feed us and tend the fire. Our youngest litter – Varjak, Jay, Jethro and Jerome – have hardly seen her. They barely even know what she looks like. She would only let that happen if she was ill, very ill. And now this Gentleman. What we saw today confirms my fears. The Contessa is gone.'

'Yes, she's probably gone somewhere,' said Father. 'I'm sure she'll be back. And in the meantime, her Gentleman friend is looking after us.'

'He is not her friend,' said the Elder Paw. 'I remember him. He came to this house years ago,

26

before any of you were born. He and the Contessa had a terrible argument. He wanted to take us away, but she wouldn't let him. She threw him out in the end, shouting and screaming.'

It was silent for a moment. Varjak saw Father's eyes glint green in the dark. There was no light in the room but the crackling, flickering fire.

'This is absurd,' said Aunt Juni. She licked her plump paws confidently. 'We're pure-bred Mesopotamian Blues, the noblest of cats. Nothing bad can happen to us.'

'It's silly to alarm the kittens like this,' tutted Mother. 'They're too young and impressionable to understand anything so serious. They'll go and have nightmares now, you see if they don't.'

'That's right.' Father arched his back and stood up. 'I don't understand the problem. The Gentleman is feeding us better than the Contessa ever did—'

'But why is he being so nice to us?' said the Elder Paw. 'Fancy food, presents – it's too good to be true. And what about those black cats who gave Varjak a scare?'

'We all know about Varjak and his tales,' declared Father. 'No, I see nothing to worry about. I don't believe in those cats, I don't believe the Contessa is dead, and I don't believe this is the same Gentleman the Elder Paw remembers. He must be getting confused in his old age.'

There was a murmur of agreement around the room. Varjak couldn't stop himself. He had to speak.

'I saw the men carry something away,' he said. 'It could've been the Contessa's body—'

'Varjak!' hissed Mother. 'That really is too revolting!' She turned to the Elder Paw. 'You see what you've done?'

'But it's true!' said Varjak. 'And so are the cats! They're—'

'Shut up, you stupid insect!' snarled Julius. 'We're the only cats in the Contessa's house. And this is grown-up business, not kitten make-believe.'

Everyone started to shout at once. The flames roared louder and higher in the fireplace.

'Listen to me!' demanded the Elder Paw, struggling to regain control. 'We need to make a plan. If things change in this house, we will have to go Outside.'

'Elder Paw!' cried Mother. 'What can you be thinking of? Everyone knows the world Outside is full of monsters. At least here we're safe from dogs.'

'But we don't even know what dogs are!' said the Elder Paw. 'This house is the only world we know.'

'This house is the only world we need,' said Aunt Juni. 'The Contessa is fine. Everything will go on as before.'

'Listen to me,' pleaded the Elder Paw. He

stepped down off the armchair and into the middle of the room.

Father squared up to him. 'No. You listen to me for a change.' His fur bristled. 'Maybe it's time for someone else to make the decisions in this family.'

The room was completely still now, except for the raging fire. Shocked at what he was seeing, but unable to look away, Varjak watched the two of them intently. Everyone did.

Father began to circle the Elder Paw, wordless and menacing. He bared his teeth. He looked twice as big, twice as fierce as normal. His shadow danced across the Elder Paw's body in the firelight. He hissed, and strode forwards.

The Elder Paw backed away. Suddenly he looked tired and old, very old, like the threadbare rug on which he stood. 'I'm just saying we should think—'

'That's enough!' blazed Father. 'This Council is over.' He turned to face the family. 'Let's go.'

There was a rumble of support around the room. Varjak's throat felt dry. He couldn't believe how fast it had happened. One moment, the Elder Paw was in charge; the next, it was all over.

'Pure-bred Mesopotamian Blues,' croaked the Elder Paw. 'The family of Jalal. Is this what we've sunk to?'

'The Council,' spat Father, 'is over.'

Chapter Four

The moment the grown-ups had left the room, Julius turned to Varjak.

'I know why the Contessa's not here,' he said, digging a claw into the toy mouse. 'It's because she can't stand to look at Varjak's eyes.'

Jasmine, Jay, Jethro and Jerome all stood by Julius's side. No one stood by Varjak's side. He was alone and boxed in by the Contessa's empty armchair.

'Poor Varjak,' said cousin Jasmine, but she was smiling as if it was some kind of joke. 'Why do you always pick on him? I'm sure he'd rather have green eyes, like everyone else!'

'Because they're different,' said Jay.

'The colour of danger,' added Jethro.

'He's not one of us,' concluded Jerome.

Varjak ignored them. He didn't even look at them, staring instead into the fire. 'The Contessa's not here because she's probably dead. Didn't you hear the Elder Paw?'

'That's enough, insect,' snapped Julius. 'No one asked you. And how dare you speak in Family Council? You're a disgrace to the name of Jalal.'

Julius's tail thudded menacingly on the rug. Very slowly, Varjak looked up and met his big brother's eyes. His own tail started to thud.

'Is that supposed to scare me?' sneered Julius. He towered over Varjak Paw. His claws came out. So did Varjak's.

'Fight! Fight! Fight!' Jay, Jethro and Jerome crowded round the two of them. Jasmine watched, grooming her fine silver-blue fur.

Varjak shook inside, but he didn't show it, didn't back off. He'd never had a real fight, and he knew he didn't stand a chance against Julius – but it was as if something inside him was rising up, something old and strong and buried deep. Who did Julius think he was?

'Julius, darling, he's only a little kitten,' cooed Jasmine, in her milk-in-the-morning voice.

'He's not even a proper Mesopotamian Blue,' said Julius. He stared at Varjak with devastating green eyes. His pupils were thin slits of scorn, mocking, challenging, daring Varjak to move first.

Varjak couldn't. He couldn't even hold the gaze: it was too strong, too sure of itself. Whatever it was that had risen up within him had gone. He turned away, and backed down.

It was over.

Julius had beaten him with just one look, as Father had beaten the Elder Paw. In the fireplace, the flames sputtered, and died.

'You're the cause of all this trouble,' said Julius. 'Apologise for what you've done.'

'I'm sorry,' croaked Varjak. The words were like hot coals in his mouth.

'And don't ever do it again – or I'll break every bone in your body.'

Varjak sloped away from the front room, humiliation scorching his cheeks. *A disgrace to the name of Jalal.* That hurt the most. He didn't care what Julius thought, but Varjak had always felt close to his ancestor, always loved the tales. He couldn't bear the thought of being a disgrace to him.

You wait, he said to an imaginary Julius in his head. You just wait. One day, I'll show you.

There was no one in the hallway. It didn't matter if he was caught going out into the garden now. Things could hardly get any worse. Varjak went up to the back door, nudged the cat flap open, and slid silently out.

The garden was a dark, gloomy place, full of gnarled old trees. They'd bent back on themselves, grown inwards and locked together, making a tangled net of knotted wood. It was hard to see the sky through them.

Beyond the trees lay the stone wall that enclosed the Contessa's house and garden. It was so high that no one in the family could imagine climbing it –

even Varjak, who could sometimes make it half way up a curtain before Mother or Father shouted him down.

He drank in the cold night air, peered at the massive wall, the tangled branches – and thought he could see a thin white whisker of moon up there, far, far above.

'*Varjak.*' It was the Elder Paw. He was on his own, at the bottom of the garden, by the crumbling roots of a dying tree. Varjak padded over to join him.

'I'm sorry, Elder Paw,' he said. 'It's my fault, everything that happened – but it's true about the black cats, I swear on the name of Jalal it's true.'

His grandfather smiled sadly. 'I know that,' he replied. 'And it's not your fault, not a bit of it. It's them. They don't even want to think any more.'

They sat in silence together, in the shadow of the wall.

'Are you still going to tell me the tale of Jalal's greatest battle?' said Varjak after a while.

'Against Saliya of the North? Not tonight,' said the Elder Paw. 'I'm afraid there are more important things to tell you first. You're still young, but I don't think we have much time, and you're the only one who'll understand.'

Varjak's skin tingled beneath his fur. Even after what had happened in the Council, he was thrilled by his grandfather's words.

'I'm ready, Elder Paw,' he said.

'Then listen carefully. Jalal only knows what this Gentleman's up to – but with the Contessa gone, it's more than we can manage. We have to get help from Outside.'

'Isn't the world Outside full of monsters?' said Varjak.

'A monster's exactly what we need. A monster called a dog. The tales say they're huge, and strong enough to kill a man. Dogs fill the heart with fear, with their foul breath and deafening sound. But the tales also say Jalal could talk to them, so there must be a way to get their help, to scare this man away.'

'Mother and Father say the tales aren't true. They say they're only stories.'

'Only stories.' The Elder Paw looked at him. 'And you believe that?'

Varjak shook his head. 'No.'

'Good. Because I'm going to tell you a family secret now, an old one. It goes right back to the beginning.' Varjak's mind raced. This was the first he'd heard of any secret.

'Is it about Jalal?' he guessed.

The Elder Paw smiled in the dark. 'It is indeed. Everyone knows the tales of Jalal – but his Way is a mystery, known only to a few.'

The Way of Jalal. This was something Julius and the others knew nothing about. And the Elder Paw was telling him: him and no one else.

'The Way,' said the Elder Paw, 'has been passed down through the ages from Paw to Paw. Much of it has been forgotten over the years, lost and corrupted through time. Now only fragments remain. Perhaps the Way will help us talk to dogs; perhaps not. I do not know it all, and I fear I won't have long enough to teach you the parts I know. But it's all we have left.'

Varjak felt strangely disappointed. Now he knew there was a family secret, he wanted to know it all. What was the point of a secret which was lost? Still, something was better than nothing.

'Tell me more, Elder Paw.'

'Come closer.' Varjak bent towards him. 'Closer.' He leaned right over, so his ear was by the Elder Paw's mouth.

'There are Seven Skills in the Way of Jalal,' whispered the Elder Paw. His breath was warm in the cold night air. 'We know only three of them. Their names are these: Slow-Time. Moving Circles. Shadow-Walking.' He recited the Skills slowly, in rhythm, like poetry. 'Learn these words, and pass them on in turn.'

'Slow-Time,' said Varjak. 'Moving Circles. Shadow-Walking.' He rolled the words over his tongue like a new taste.

'Again.'

slow

time

moving

circles

shadow

walking

'Slow-Time. Moving Circles. Shadow-Walking.'
His fur prickled at the strange sounds.

'Never forget this. Keep the Way alive, Varjak Paw.'

Varjak nodded. The words – Jalal's words – were safe in his head. He would always remember them.

click

The back door swung open. Varjak and the Elder Paw looked round. The Gentleman was standing there. And by his shiny black shoes, there were two sleek black cats.

again

Chapter Five

The temperature seemed to drop. Varjak shivered.

'I don't like this,' whispered the Elder Paw. 'I don't like it one bit.'

The Gentleman pointed at them across the garden. He crouched down to touch the collars on the black cats' necks, and whispered something into their ears. Then he turned and went back inside, leaving Varjak and the Elder Paw alone with his cats.

Varjak's fur bushed out with fear as the cats came slowly, deliberately across the grass towards them. There was something so strange, so menacing about the way they moved.

'Who are you?' called the Elder Paw.

They didn't answer. They just kept coming. Varjak and his grandfather backed away, but there wasn't far to go. In a few steps, they were up against the wall, as far from the house as they could get.

Varjak's pulse was racing. He remembered how the Gentleman's cats had pushed him aside so easily. It looked like nothing in the world could stop them now. He scratched at his collar. It felt tight around his neck.

'Varjak,' said the Elder Paw urgently, but without a hint of worry in his voice, 'I think someone as brave as you could climb this wall and go Outside, don't you?'

Varjak glanced up. The stone was concealed by moss, but there was no hiding the wall's height. It was massive.

'Don't worry,' said the Elder Paw. 'You'll have time. I'll see to that.'

'*I'll* have time?' Varjak's head swam. What was the Elder Paw saying? That he should go Outside on his own? 'But – can't we both—?'

'No, we can't. Only one of us can get out. I'll keep them busy; you must go Outside and find a dog.'

'You're not going to fight them, are you? They'll – they'll—'

The Elder Paw took a pace towards the black cats. In his eyes was a fire Varjak had never seen before.

'Go! Bring back this thing that even men are scared of. And keep the Way alive, Varjak Paw.'

The cats had stopped. They were looking at the Elder Paw as if they were waiting for him. The Elder Paw growled at them. Varjak's head hurt. He was being torn apart by a thousand different feelings.

The Elder Paw strode forward to meet the Gentleman's cats, tail held high, green eyes blazing. 'Go, Varjak, before it's too late. Don't look back. This is the only way.' He looked fierce and magnificent. The tired old cat of the Council was gone. Now he was a son of Jalal, facing his enemy, proud and powerful. A Mesopotamian Blue.

'GO!' he yelled, and hurled himself at the black cats.

They nodded as he came, as if it was all too easy. The Elder Paw ran straight at them – but then he seemed to shimmer for a moment, and went through the gap between them, and came out the other side.

The two black cats span around. The Elder Paw was just out of their reach. They glanced at each other, and went after him.

Varjak's heart thumped in his throat. His grandfather was leading them away, through the trees, back towards the house. He was taking them further and further from Varjak, with quick wits and cunning, a flash of silver blue.

The black cats were faster. They moved together perfectly. Each one looked sleek and lethal. How could the Elder Paw fight two together? Already he was slowing down; still proud, but old and short of breath. And the black cats were closing in, one on each side.

They'd catch him soon. Even if they didn't, what could he do against a Gentleman ten times his size? What could any cat do, or even a whole family?

The Elder Paw was right. The only chance was to find a dog. His grandfather was doing what he had to; now it was all up to Varjak.

His mind on fire, Varjak tore his eyes from the garden, and turned to the wall. It separated the world he knew from the world Outside. No Paw had been over that wall since Jalal himself came from Mesopotamia, but it was the only way out.

He took a deep breath, coiled his body tight. One last glance, over his shoulder. No!

The black cats had caught the Elder Paw. They had him backed against the house. They came at him from both sides. He slashed out, but together they swarmed on top of him, and forced him to the ground.

There was a terrible howl. The black cats came away, shaking their heads. And the Elder Paw—

The Elder Paw looked limp, like a broken toy.

There was a roaring in Varjak's ears. His stomach

churned. Everything inside him screamed at him to stay, to fight, to help the only cat who ever understood him. But the Elder Paw's words echoed in his mind: *go, before it's too late.* He turned to the wall.

Three.

Two.

One.

Varjak exploded into motion. Back legs uncoiled. Front paws reached out for a grip. Found it. Back legs pushed, pumped, powered up, up, and like the wind, Varjak Paw flew up the face of the wall, up, through the trees, higher than the curtains, higher than the house, up, beginning to tire, muscles aching, vision blurring – how much further? – up, grip after grip, paw over paw, slipping . . .

Latched onto a ledge. Heaved.
And made it to the top of the wall.

Outside! For the first time since Jalal,
a Paw stood on the edge of the world.

Chapter Six

Varjak could see for miles and miles. There were no walls or trees to block his view any more.

Just open space, rippling out ahead of him, beneath him, above him. He was standing in space, and it was a long way to fall.

He peered down the inside of the wall. He could see nothing through the trees. The Gentleman's cats and the Elder Paw were hidden by the tangled net of branches. There was no way back. He was truly on his own.

Had he done the right thing? Shouldn't he have helped his grandfather? He couldn't get that picture out of his mind: the Elder Paw, limp, like a broken toy.

Tremors were coming up from somewhere deep within him, racking him open. Varjak blocked them, stopped them, pushed them back down. The Elder Paw knew what he was doing. He'd planned it. He was willing to lay down his life, so Varjak could have the chance to go Outside, and find a dog.

All he could do now was go on. But where?

Ahead of him was a sea of lights, stretching far away into the darkness. Varjak couldn't tell what they were, or where they led. He looked up. Another sea of lights: the moon and stars, cold and distant. They made him giddy in the pit of his stomach, so dizzy that he could almost feel the wall slip out from under him.

He closed his eyes and counted to ten. It didn't work. The view was too big; he was too small. A pure-bred Mesopotamian Blue had no place on top of a wall. But then, as his family said, he wasn't much of a Blue. So who was he?

Beneath that giant sky, he was no one. He was nothing.

Varjak's stomach lurched. He was going to be sick if he stayed on the wall any longer. Down. He had to get down, and quickly – the black cats would be looking for him. But how? He couldn't climb down the wall: it was sheer. He'd over-balance and crash if he tried.

There was a tree Outside the wall, just one. He could climb down a tree, if he could only make it that far.

He stretched out a paw. His pad zipped on the wet moss that cloaked the stone. He clung on with his claws and regained his balance. A blast of bitterly cold wind almost pushed him over the edge. Another wave of giddiness washed over him. The wind seemed to taunt him with its song. *Too high*, it sang. *Too high, too soon!* Varjak tried to shut it out, but the song was everywhere. *You've gone too high too soon. You'll never make it to that tree!*

He ignored it, positioned his tail for extra balance and took another step along the mossy stone. It was like walking on ice: treacherous: impossible. In his mind, he saw himself slip, slide, skid off that wall, smash to pieces on the ground below. He shuddered.

Think of something else, he told himself. Think of the Way. What was it? Slow-Time. Moving Circles.

Shadow-Walking.

Varjak staggered towards the tree. *Too high,* whistled the wind.

'Slow-Time!' he yelled back. He wasn't going to let the wind beat him.

'Moving Circles!' He wasn't going to let the wall beat him.

'Shadow-Walking!' Because he was Varjak Paw, and he knew the Way.

Varjak walked the wall like he'd been walking walls all his life. He was light and springy on his paws. It worked: the Way actually worked! He wasn't dizzy any more. He didn't feel sick.

I'd like to see Julius do this, he thought.

Now he just had to step into the tree, and he could climb down easily. He'd done the hard part. Varjak grinned, and pounced onto the nearest branch.

CRACK!
Falling . . .
Didn't test it? Stupid!

The wind whipped into his face as he fell towards the ground. He closed his eyes –

– and everything went black.

Chapter Seven

Varjak dreamed.

He dreamed he was walking by a river in the heat of the night. Zigzag trees swayed in the warm breeze. The air smelled like cinnamon, and tasted of ripe dates. He looked up. The stars were different. They sparkled big and bright in a brilliant sky.

An old cat with silver-blue fur like starlight walked beside him. He looked like a Mesopotamian Blue, but he wore no collar and his eyes were amber like the rising sun.

'Welcome to the land of your ancestors,' said the old cat. 'Welcome to Mesopotamia.'

'Mesopotamia? Where Jalal came from?'

'Jalal the Paw, yes indeed. This was his home in olden days.'

Varjak's pulse beat a little faster. 'Did you know Jalal?' he said.

'And if I did?'

'Then I'd ask you questions! Are the tales true?

Could he really talk to dogs? And – and what would he think of me?'

The old cat cackled. 'What a question! Why should that matter to you?'

Varjak looked away. 'My family say I'm a disgrace to the name of Jalal. They say I'm not a proper, pure-bred Mesopotamian Blue.'

'Oh? And what say you? Are you worthy of your ancestors – or not?'

'No,' said Varjak quietly. He hung his head. 'I'm not.'

'What if you knew the secret Way of Jalal? Would you then be a proper, pure-bred Mesopotamian Blue?'

Varjak smiled sadly, remembering the Elder Paw. 'I already know about the Way. And I feel just the same.'

'You know the Way? How impressive. Perhaps you will demonstrate. Strike me.'

The old cat stopped walking. He blocked Varjak's path. He wasn't big, but something about him looked dangerous. Varjak stepped back a pace.

'Strike me!' he commanded again. His amber eyes flashed. 'Strike me now, or die where you stand.'

Well, if that was what he wanted . . . why not?

Varjak swiped gently at the mad old cat, meaning to tap him on the side. But somehow, he didn't connect. His paw sailed through the air, and thudded harmlessly on the ground. Varjak frowned. How could he have missed?

The old cat combed his whiskers. 'Am I too quick for you?' he challenged. 'Is this the Way of Jalal? I think you know nothing, little kitten. Strike me again!'

This was becoming annoying. Now Varjak wanted to hit him, hit him hard. He decided to give it his best shot: there was no way he could miss.

He slammed out a silver-blue paw, missed completely, and lost his balance. Those alien stars twinkled at him with silent laughter as he rolled onto the riverbank. He sprang up again, furious.

'Once more!' goaded the old cat. Varjak's frustration boiled over. He lashed out. His paw flapped stupidly in space, and he toppled to the ground. He kicked with his back legs, but he was fighting himself now, and he knew it.

He was beaten.

His elderly opponent peered down at him. 'I thought the first attack rather half-hearted,' he said, as if they were having a friendly chat about the weather. 'The third was crude and clumsy, as you know. The second showed potential, yes; but it was slow, terribly slow . . . Still, you have spirit. If you wish to learn the Way – the true Way – only ask, and I will teach you.'

Varjak couldn't speak. The words stuck in his throat. He felt ashamed and embarrassed. It was obvious that this old cat knew far more about the Way than him, but he couldn't bring himself to admit it. His pride wouldn't allow it.

The old cat shrugged. 'Farewell, then.' He began to walk away.

Something shifted inside Varjak, like a locked door opening. 'Wait!' he called. The old cat turned about. His body shimmered in the warm breeze. 'Don't go,' said Varjak. 'I – I want to learn the Way.'

The old cat smiled. 'Very well. Then I shall teach you. We begin now.' He cleared his throat. 'There are Seven Skills in the Way of Jalal. The First of these is Open Mind, and you have just found its secret. For only when you admit that you know nothing, can you truly know anything.'

Varjak's eyes widened as the words sank in. 'Who are you?'

'Do you still not know me, my son?'

'Jalal?'

'Jalal the Paw, that am I.' He winked. 'Believe none of the tales.'

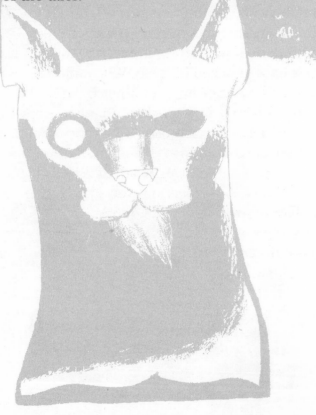

Chapter Eight

Varjak awoke at the foot of the wall. His head was pounding, his paws aching. It wasn't quite light yet, but the night was almost over. The fall from the tree must have knocked him out. What a dream! He wondered if he'd ever have another like it.

He shivered. It was cold out in the open, and the grass beneath his body was wet. He stood up, shook the moisture from his fur, and looked around.

The view cleared his head instantly. Outside was like nothing he'd seen, or even dreamed of.

The Contessa's house stood on top of a high hill. Beneath it was a broad, green park. Beyond it, away in the distance, was a city.

Stretched out under the open sky, shining like silver in the pre-dawn light, the city was a huge, mad jumble of shapes and sizes. It had tall towers, gleaming steel and glass – but also squat brick houses, dark with chimney smoke. Wide open gardens jostled with narrow alleys; sharp pointy spires topped soft, curved domes; concrete blocks loomed over bright painted billboards.

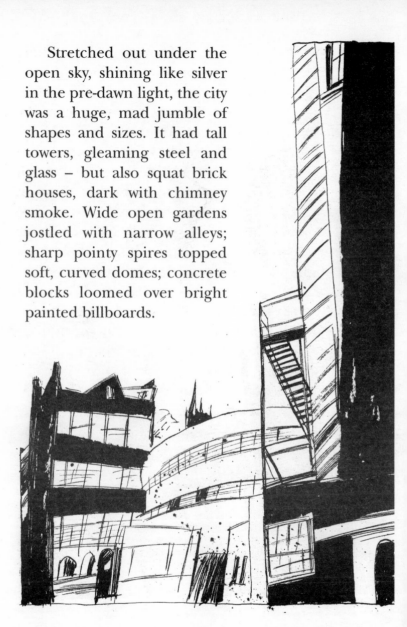

They were all in there together, side by side, each one part of the whole. There was so much, he couldn't take it in. All he could hear from here was the wind rustling through the treetops, but down in the city it looked noisy and bustling, a place that never went to sleep.

His whiskers twitched with a mix of energy, excitement, danger. His heart beat faster, just looking at it. It seemed like a city where anything could happen, and probably did. A place you could do whatever you liked, and no one would stop you. Where you'd be able to find everything you wanted – even a dog.

The terror of the night before, the fight with the Gentleman's cats: it seemed a long time ago, and very far away. There was sadness in his heart for the Elder Paw, deep sadness, but his grandfather had trusted him with a mission. It was his duty as a Blue to save the family, and Varjak intended to see it through.

He ventured down the hill. It was steeper than it looked, and soon he found himself running, almost rolling down the slope. But it was joy to stretch out in the open. A splash of sunshine lit the horizon. He'd never seen a sunrise before, and the sky Outside was alive with streaks of amber light.

The sky flashed past his eyes as he sped up, sprinted to the bottom. He bounded over a fence at the foot of the hill and into the park.

Around this time, back in the Contessa's house, the family would be waking up and licking each other clean. Varjak grinned. He hated washing, and already there was a satisfying build-up of mud between his claws.

Next, the family would obediently munch their food out of china bowls. It would be the Gentleman's vile-smelling caviare today. But now that he was Outside, he wouldn't have to eat anything he didn't like. He could choose what to eat and when to eat.

After eating, the family would go to their litter trays. Ha! Varjak crouched by a tree. No litter tray for him today. It felt good; it felt natural. It felt, he thought, like it ought to feel.

This was how it would be in the future. It was going to be the best time of his life. He'd return from the city with a dog (whatever a dog was) and defeat the Gentleman and his strange black cats. Then he'd lead his family out of that stuffy old house into this wonderful new world. They'd all say he was a proper Mesopotamian Blue, a true son of Jalal. They'd offer him every kind of honour and reward, but he'd turn them down. 'I did it for the glory of the family,' he'd say humbly, and they would cheer him even more.

Varjak wandered further and further in his happy daze. He barely noticed the fiery shades of sunrise burn out, leaving a sky the colour of cold ashes.

A violent sound cut through his thoughts. It was like shrieking and roaring at the same time, and it scared him. The sound came from a black road that circled the park in the distance. He crept towards it, ears pressed against his skull. And then he saw them.

It was a column of fearsome monsters. They were rolling down the road, roaring at each other and everything around them. Huge monsters made of metal with sharp edges all around. They had yellow eyes at the front and red eyes at the back. They moved on round black wheels which turned so fast it made Varjak dizzy, and they belched a trail of choking smoke behind them on the wind.

Could these be dogs?

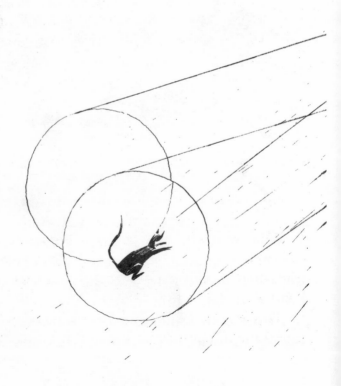

What were the Elder Paw's words? These monsters were big enough to kill a man. Their breath was foul; their sound was deafening. And they filled his heart with fear.

This was it. He was sure they were dogs. He'd found them.

A hard, tight ball of terror formed in Varjak's stomach. How was he supposed to talk to these monsters? They didn't look as if they'd stop for anyone, let alone a kitten. As he edged closer to the procession of metal beasts, all his happy thoughts about the future faded like a false sunrise.

Slow-Time. Moving Circles. Shadow-Walking.

He shook his head. How were those words supposed to help? Why had the Elder Paw trusted him with such an impossible mission? Why hadn't he chosen someone older and stronger, someone like Julius? Julius might know what to do with a dog; Varjak did not.

The quest was too hard. It was impossible. The ball of terror in his stomach turned into a heavy lump of despair.

A drop of rain splattered on his shoulder. Varjak grimaced. He hated water on his fur. At home, he would rush in through the cat door as soon as the weather changed. If only he could do that now. He glanced at the high hill behind him. He couldn't see the house from here.

A gust of wind sliced across his face. The sky darkened. A storm was coming: he could feel it.

Shelter. That was what he needed. Once he was safe from the storm, he could think about the dogs. But there was no shelter in this wide open park. There were only trees, solitary trees with no leaves, swaying in the wind. They wouldn't keep him warm and dry.

The sky darkened. The wind cut through his coat. Varjak could clearly see each blade of grass, each fallen leaf, trembling alone before the storm. Shelter. He had to find shelter, and fast.

Rain came down from the darkening sky: thick, wet rain that dripped into his fur, weighing him down with water. He tried to shake it off, but once it started, the rain kept coming. His family were right. Outside was no place for a cat. It was no place at all.

In the distance, behind the naked, shivering trees, he glimpsed something that he'd missed before. A small, wooden hut. A shelter!

He fought his way towards it. The rain whipped into his eyes. The wind pushed him back one step for every two he took. The ground was turning into a churning sea of mud. His paws slipped and sloshed wildly.

SPLASH! Varjak fell into a pool of oozing mud. Dark, dirty water seeped out of his mouth. He was covered in brown and green slime. He could feel it squelching all around him, soaking into his skin. The wind howled at him like a wounded animal. *Too far*, it howled, *you've gone too far.*

A claw of white light slashed the belly of the sky. There was a moment of horrible silence, and then the earth juddered with thunder, shaking beneath him as if it would break in two.

'Help me, Jalal!' he cried. But only the sky answered, bellowing again with angry thunder, making him wish he hadn't spoken.

Varjak wiped the slime from his eyes and dragged himself to the hut. It smelled of soggy timber and had no windows, only a door. The door was closed. He pushed. It moved, but only a crack. Desperate, he flung himself at the flimsy wood that stood between him and shelter from the storm – and the door swung open.

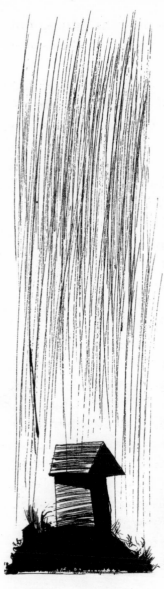

Chapter Nine

It was dark as midnight in the hut. It felt close and damp, but at least inside was drier than Outside. Varjak was safe at last. He relaxed. And then a low growl ripped the air.

The door slammed shut behind him.

'Don't move a muscle,' said a gravelly voice. 'You're surrounded.'

Varjak's claws slid out, ready to fight. 'Put those claws away,' commanded the voice.

Varjak opened his eyes wide. It was another cat! She had spiky black-and-white fur and mustard-coloured eyes. She looked about the same age as him; younger than Jasmine or Julius, but harder, as if she'd seen too much of the world already.

'I'm not looking for a fight,' she said, 'but if you don't put the claws away, I'll rip you to shreds.' Something in her gravelly voice left Varjak in no doubt that she meant it.

'I'm not looking for a fight either,' he said, and put away his claws. The rain thudded on the roof of the hut like a nervous heartbeat.

'OK,' she said. 'This is my hut, my shelter. Everyone knows that. What are you doing here?'

Varjak glanced at the door. 'It's raining.'

'And?'

'And this was the only shelter I could find.'

'Can't you see it's taken?' she growled.

'Isn't it big enough for both of us?'

'There's only room for one.'

That certainly wasn't true, but Varjak didn't think she'd appreciate him saying it. He stared silently at the soggy timber floor. A puddle had already formed around him. He couldn't face going out again. Besides, she was the only cat he'd met since leaving home. She was nothing like a Mesopotamian Blue, but she wasn't like the Gentleman's cats either. There was nothing strange or scary about her – though you wouldn't want her for an enemy.

Varjak tried to smile through the dark at her.

She glared back.

'What's your name?' she said gruffly. 'I haven't seen you round here before.'

'It's Varjak Paw.'

'Varjak Paw?' she said. 'Varjak Paw? What kind of a name is that?'

What was wrong with his name? 'What's yours?'

'None of your business. Whose gang are you with? Who's your Boss? Are you running from the Vanishings?'

Varjak hesitated. What did all these questions mean? He didn't know – but he had to say something.

He blurted out the first thing that came to mind: something he didn't even believe himself. 'I'm a pure-bred Mesopotamian Blue.'

'A what?'

'A Mesopotamian Blue. We're very rare. Special cats.'

'*Special?*' she spluttered. 'I don't care how pure-bred you are, or where you think you're from. The only thing that counts is what you do.'

A blast of thunder rattled the hut. Varjak frowned. He'd never heard anyone talk like that before.

'What kind of cat are you?' he asked.

'I'm asking the questions, Special Cat,' she said. She sounded disgusted. 'Now tell me what you *really* do. Are you one of Ginger's gang? Or are you with Sally Bones?'

Keep talking, that was the best thing. 'I told you, I'm a Mesopotamian Blue. We live on the hill.'

She sighed, and tapped her claws on the floor. 'Everyone knows there's no food up there. Even the gangs don't bother with it. Come on, tell the truth. You must be with a gang, or a little cat like you'd be starving by now.'

Her words sent a shiver down Varjak's spine. How could she not know about the Contessa's house? This world Outside and the world he came from seemed completely cut off from each other.

'Listen,' she said, 'if you're so high and mighty, how come you're out in the park in a storm?'

'I'm Outside because I need to talk to a dog,' he said. She stared at him as if she didn't understand. 'Dogs are huge, noisy monsters,' he explained.

'I know what a dog is,' she snapped.

Then maybe she could help. 'Do you know how to talk to them?'

She scowled, like she couldn't believe what she was hearing.

'I know it sounds strange,' said Varjak. 'But I've got to do it, to save my family. They're in a lot of danger.'

The black-and-white cat laughed out loud. 'He thinks he can talk to a dog!' Even her laugh sounded like the crunch of gravel. Varjak scratched an itch

73

under his collar. It felt uncomfortable.

'What's that you're scratching?' she said.

'My collar?'

'Collar . . .' A strange expression crossed her face; and then she seemed to relax. 'Isn't that what pets wear?'

Varjak peered at her own neck. She wore no collar.

'Yes, now it makes sense,' she said. 'You're just a pet cat who's got lost in the storm, aren't you? You're not in a gang. You don't know about the Vanishings. You don't know anything about this city at all, do you?'

Varjak almost denied it. Then he remembered his dream. Open Mind, the First Skill: *only when you admit that you know nothing, can you truly know anything.*

'All I know is that I need your help,' he said quietly. 'I need a place to stay until the storm's over, and then I've got to find a dog.'

She looked into his eyes for a long time. The rain

beat down, relentless. 'All right, pet cat,' she said at last. 'You can stay. Just till the rain stops, and then you go. Understand?'

Varjak smiled. 'Thanks.'

'Just don't talk to me about dogs, that's all,' she muttered.

They sat together in the darkness. Varjak was bursting with questions. Were there many other cats Outside? What were these gangs and Vanishings she kept talking about? And how, exactly, *did* you talk to a dog?

There were so many new things to understand. But the black-and-white cat was curled up into a spiky ball. Any more words would breach the invisible barrier she'd made between them.

The rain went on. Varjak shivered. He was cold and tired. His eyelids drooped. He tried to force them open, but they kept closing by themselves. It would be madness to fall asleep in a strange place with a strange cat, but he couldn't help it.

He slept in his corner of the hut, still shivering as the rainwater and slime dripped from his muddy fur.

Chapter Ten

Varjak dreamed.

He dreamed he was back in Mesopotamia. Zigzag trees swayed in the warm night breeze. The sky was bright with stars. The air smelled like cinnamon and tasted of ripe dates.

Jalal walked beside him.

'Can you teach me how to talk to dogs, Jalal?'

'What kind of trees are these?' said the old cat abruptly.

'Trees?'

'All around us, there are trees. Perhaps you have noticed?'

The zigzag trees: Varjak nodded.

'So, what kind of trees are they, Varjak Paw?'

Varjak bit his tongue. Jalal wasn't talking about dogs, and Varjak had no idea about the trees. He didn't want to disappoint his ancestor, but what else could he do? 'I don't know,' he admitted.

Jalal stopped walking, and placed his paws squarely on the earth. 'Awareness,' he said. 'The Second Skill. If you are to survive in the world, you must be aware of everything in it. Whether you need to find food, fight an enemy, or even talk to a dog – before you do anything, you must know what you are dealing with. Assume nothing; be sure of the facts. Open your senses. Spread them wide, like a net. Observe the world: what it looks like, what it sounds like. Even what it tastes like.'

'The air tastes of dates,' suggested Varjak.

'It does indeed. That is because these trees are date palms. See the zigzag patterns on the trunk? That is how to recognize a date palm tree.'

Jalal pointed out the other trees on the riverbank.

He gave names to the trees, and taught Varjak how to recognize them by the patterns on their trunks and the scents of their fruits. Varjak stored the knowledge carefully in his mind as they stood under the palms, practising Awareness, for a timeless time.

'Again,' Jalal always said. He was a stern teacher. 'Again.' And then, at last, 'Enough.'

'I never knew there was so much in the world,' said Varjak.

'That is because until now, you have used only a small part of your potential. The rest is locked within you. But you are capable of anything, my son, anything at all. Each sense is like a fine web that goes out into the world. Your whiskers can detect the slightest changes in the air, the smallest movements. Your nose can scent fear. Once developed, your Awareness can even feel danger, and tell you when you are being watched.' Jalal's ears suddenly pricked up. He dropped into a low crouch. 'Listen! Can you hear it?'

Varjak listened to the peaceful Mesopotamian

night. He could hear nothing unusual.

'Pay attention!' said Jalal. 'Near the top of the range, there is a scratching, squeaking, chirping noise. It comes from the edge of the water. Can you hear it now?'

Varjak closed his eyes, and concentrated. There it was, just as Jalal said.

'I hear it. But what is it?'

'Breakfast,' said Jalal.

Chapter Eleven

'Hey!' Varjak heard the gravelly voice as if from a great distance. 'Hey, you! Poor Jack, or whatever your name is! Wake up!'

He opened his eyes. Once again, the dream was over. He was back in the soggy timber hut, in the middle of the park. He was cold. Wet. And hungry.

'Did you say something about breakfast?' he groaned. He heaved himself up and scratched his ear. A trail of dirty water trickled out.

'Breakfast?' said another voice. Varjak looked to the door. It was open. A comfortable-looking cat with shaggy, chocolate-brown fur sat there. 'I haven't heard that word for a long time,' she said. 'Remember breakfast, Holly?'

The spiky black-and-white cat called Holly shook her head. 'Did you find anything?' she asked.

'Not a sausage – but looks like you have.' The new cat winked at Varjak. 'Where'd you dig him up?'

'Mind your own business,' said Holly. She turned to Varjak. 'The storm's over. It's time to go.'

He peered through the door. It was night again. It looked freezing out there. He had a memory flash: the sky bellowing with thunder. He couldn't stand to be alone so soon.

'Have a heart, Holly,' said the chocolate-brown cat. 'Look at him, he's obviously not dangerous.' She smiled at Varjak. 'My name's Tam. Don't you mind Holly here. She's in a bad mood right now, but her bark's worse than her bite.'

'That's enough,' snapped Holly. Varjak looked into her eyes. They were a sharp mustard colour.

'So, are you going to help me find a dog?' he asked.

'A dog?' said Tam. Her eyes were wide and round, like saucers. 'Why?'

'I need to talk to one.'

'Talk to a dog?' Tam whispered.

'I know it's difficult—'

Her shaggy coat shuddered. 'It's worse than that! Do you have any idea what you're saying?'

'Don't listen to him, Tam,' said Holly. 'He does-n't know anything.'

'Yes I do!' said Varjak.

'Go on, tell Tam what your name is.' She smiled.

'I'm Varjak Paw,' he said, with all the dignity he could muster. 'It's a noble name; I'm a Mesopotamian Blue.'

There was hush for a moment, and then Tam started to giggle. Holly grinned.

'Messsuppa what?' said Tam.

'Mesopotamia. It's where my family's from.'

'Sounds weird,' said Tam. 'Where is it?'

Varjak scratched his head. 'I don't exactly know,' he admitted, 'but—'

'Haven't you been there?'

'I've only ever dreamed about it.'

They both laughed this time. The strange thing was, Varjak didn't mind. It wasn't like being bullied by Julius. These cats were so different from his family. He enjoyed the way they talked, even when they teased him. He grinned with them, and just for a moment, he felt the invisible barrier between them drop.

'Well then,' Tam said, 'if you're not from there, you're from here. You're one of us.'

'He's not from here,' Holly told her. 'He's a pet. Says he lives on the hill, got lost in the storm.'

'I'm here to save my family,' said Varjak.

'You are?' breathed Tam. 'From who?'

'A Gentleman. He's got these scary black cats – even their eyes are black. And they walk all strange.' Varjak paused. He knew he was sounding odd. 'Like this,' he said, and tried to walk like the black cats, but found he couldn't really do it on his own. Tam and Holly cracked up laughing again.

'I like him,' said Tam. 'He reminds me of Luka.'

The warm laughter died away all of a sudden, and the hut became very silent. Varjak looked over at Holly. There was a sad look in her mustard eyes.

'Luka's a friend of ours,' said Tam. 'He used to be. He looked like me, but he sounded like you; he could always make us laugh. Anyway, he ended up joining a gang. It was when the food started to run out – the gangs were taking everything. We were so hungry.'

'I told him it was a bad idea,' said Holly, quietly, 'but he joined one anyway. And then he Vanished. Some friend.'

'He left you?' asked Varjak.

'Not left,' said Holly. 'Vanished. It happens all the time in this city.' She glanced at the door. Her invisible barrier was definitely up again. 'But that's just what friends do. They're not worth having.'

'Why not?' Varjak thought he'd give anything and do anything for a friend. Nothing could be worth more.

'Because they let you down. They leave you in the end. It's best to be alone.'

'Don't worry, Varjak,' said Tam. 'She doesn't mean it. Holly tries to act all hard, but she's the

best friend you could have. And she likes you really
– I can tell.'

'That's enough!' shouted Holly. She looked hurt.
'If you two are such good friends now, why don't you
just go off together?'

She stalked away, out of the hut, into the park.
She was going. Varjak followed her. He had a strange
feeling, like something important was slipping
through his paws.

'Wait—' he said.

'Don't follow me,' she growled as she padded off,
tail held up, spiky and solitary. An unapproachable
cat.

'Oh, no,' said Tam, hurrying after her. 'I shouldn't
have mentioned Luka. I ruined it. Holly, wait for
me!' She scuttled away into the night.

And Varjak Paw was alone once again.

Chapter Twelve

Varjak walked in the other direction. He shivered as he walked. The grass felt wet and clammy cold beneath his paws. The sky was clear after the storm, but it looked hollow and black, as though the rain had washed even the moon and stars away.

It was much worse being alone now that he'd had a moment with Holly and Tam. It made him realize how alone he'd been before, and how lonely he was again now. Still, he had to get on with his mission: find a dog, take it home, beat the Gentleman and his cats.

The city loomed up ahead. From the hill he'd seen it all, and how it fitted together. But on ground level, he couldn't see further than the nearest building. Even the smallest of them blocked his way. Their thick brick walls reared up before him, higher than the Contessa's house.

The night was full of strange sounds too. Things were rumbling, bells ringing, sirens wailing. What did it all mean? How was he going to find his way through it? He badly needed help. Holly and Tam seemed to know what they were doing – but they were gone, and they weren't coming back.

Varjak walked through a gate at the park's edge. Beyond it was a narrow pavement and a wide black road, lined by orange street lamps. They looked like spiny iron trees, with clusters of light on their branches. Instead of the sweet scent of fruit, they smelled sharp and electric, buzzing nervously above him.

He felt exposed in their glare. Further down the pavement, he could hear people, groups of them. Some were talking, others were laughing or shouting at each other. His fur prickled, remembering the men who came to the Contessa's house that night.

He didn't want to be seen; it felt too risky out here on his own. Across the road, there was a quiet-looking alleyway between the brick houses. It looked a safer place to be.

Varjak stepped onto the pavement – and froze in his tracks. Before him, lined up on the edge of the road, was a whole column of shiny metal monsters. They stood in single file, stock still. They weren't moving, or making any sound. Their eyes were dull and lightless, their round black wheels at rest.

But they were dogs – and this was Varjak's chance to talk to them.

'Excuse me,' he said.

They didn't react; not even a flicker in the eyes. Perhaps they were sleeping. He took a deep breath, and crept closer to them, ready to run if they suddenly awoke. He slunk onto the road, stretched out a paw, and gingerly touched a monster's smooth metal flank.

It was cold. Not asleep, but dead. Varjak shivered at the thought.

Far away, but closing in, something shrieked. Something roared. Varjak's heart thudded in his chest as he turned to face it. The shrieking, roaring noise grew louder. It was a pack of dogs, live ones, and they were coming down the road towards him.

He'd forgotten how fast and wild they were. In motion, they blurred beneath the street lights. Their yellow eyes were open, so round and bright they seemed to pierce his skull. He couldn't meet their gaze.

He had to look away. No wonder people were scared of them!

Varjak quaked as the monsters roared past, one after another after another. They were massive, mighty, unstoppable. In their wake came that foul, choking smell. It made him cough and cough and cough.

He cowered in the lethal wind; watched the red eyes at the back recede into the distance.

What should I do, Jalal?

Awareness, the Second Skill: *before you do anything, you must know what you are dealing with. Assume nothing; be sure of the facts.*

All right. The fact was, these dogs wouldn't notice him if he just sat there and called out to them. They wouldn't even hear him. He had to make one of them stop. That came first.

There was only one way to do it, and Varjak's stomach tightened as he realized what it meant. He was going to have to stand in front of them, in the middle of the road, as they sped towards him. Then they'd see him and would have no choice but to stop.

It would take courage, but he could do it. He could do it. He was sure he could.

Deep inside him, something shrugged its shoulders and walked away. Absolutely not, it said. I'm not Jalal. I'm not even Julius. The dogs are never going to stop for me. Even if they see me, they'll just run me over. They'll kill me. Look at them! They're huge, heartless monsters. They don't slow down for anything. It's pointless even to try.

But he had to try. The Elder Paw gave his life so he could try: him and no one else. That sacrifice would mean nothing unless Varjak was prepared to risk his own life too. And hadn't he always wanted a chance to prove himself a proper Mesopotamian Blue?

Varjak closed his eyes. Took a deep breath. And strode out into the road, to the very centre of the dogs' path.

Another pair of yellow eyes appeared in the distance. He could smell the foul breath from here. He could hear the deafening roar. The tales were right: these monsters filled his heart with fear. It clawed at his insides as they came towards him.

'Stop!' he called.

The eyes were big and dazzling. Varjak looked straight into them. He ignored the piercing pain they made in his head. He ignored his muscles, screaming at him to run from this oncoming beast. He stood his ground.

He remembered the Elder Paw, in the garden, facing up to the Gentleman's black cats. So brave. That was what he needed now.

'Please stop!' he shouted. 'I have to talk to you!'

The eyes grew bigger. And bigger. The monster was coming closer, and closer. And behind it, he could see others of its kind: a whole pack of them. Good. He was smack in front of them. They couldn't get past without going through him.

Jalal could do this. *I can do it too.*

The monsters kept coming. And still he stood his ground, though he had to dig claws into tarmac to stop himself running.

'I need your help!' he yelled. 'Please! Please! *Please!*'

But the monsters weren't slowing. They were speeding. They were shrieking, roaring, bearing down on him. Huge, deadly. Stand your ground, stand your . . .

BRAAAAAP!
fur
fluttered
fur
flattened.
Monsters roared over his head –
– to his left –
– to his right –
– to his left –
– and were gone.

94

Varjak stayed flat on the ground, cowering, crushing himself into the tarmac, even though the dogs were gone, and all his hopes of saving the family with them.

He crawled across the hard black road to the other side, still not daring to stand up straight. His body shook with shock. If he'd moved, if he'd even breathed as they passed over him, they would have destroyed him.

He'd come within a whisker of death. He knew that. But that wasn't the worst of it.

The worst of it was that he'd failed.

Chapter Thirteen

Varjak's head hung low.

He could hear more monsters in the distance, coming closer. He couldn't face looking at them. What was the point? He knew now that they'd never stop and help him, not in a million years.

He'd failed to do the one and only thing he'd ever been trusted with. What good was he to anyone? Julius was right. He was no Mesopotamian Blue, and never would be. He was an insect. Worse than an insect, he was a disgrace to the name of Jalal.

He'd failed.

Varjak glanced up at the hill, far away on the other side of the park. There was no way he could go back there, not without a dog. That meant he might never see his home again. The kitchen full of china bowls, the Contessa's red velvet armchair, even the new toy mouse: never again.

He slunk into
an alley that led
away from the mon-
sters, away from the
hill, away from his
memories of home.

This alley was
narrow, and dark
with the shadows of
night.

It was empty except for a swarm of black plastic rubbish bags, so full that they'd split open. Ruined food seeped out of the bags like blood from a wound. The ground was slippery with scraps: soggy bread, slimy fruit, discarded and decaying in the dirt.

Somewhere in the distance, almost buried by these smells, was the tang of meat. Varjak's stomach grumbled. It had been so long since he'd eaten. He remembered insisting to Mother and Father that he wanted to hunt, like Jalal. He laughed bitterly at the memory. It was easy to talk about hunting, but to actually do it? Him, the coward who couldn't even stop a dog? Varjak, who'd disgraced his whole family, a hunter like his famous ancestor? No: an old scrap of meat was all he was good for, all he could get.

Varjak followed the scent. His Awareness led him along the alley and over a wall. He came down into the most desolate place he'd seen.

It was an enclosed courtyard. The sky was hidden here – he'd lost the moon and stars. He could see nothing but big concrete tower blocks, looming all around. Every door and window was shut, as if the people inside were trying to keep something out.

This place made him nervous. The blocks would be impossible to climb: their walls were smooth and sheer. If something went wrong, if there was trouble, he could easily be trapped. The only way out was the way he'd come in. Still, at least it was shadowy. There were plenty of places to hide. And it was quiet; all he could hear was the muffled rumbling of the city in the distance.

The smell of meat was potent in this barren place. With grim precision, Varjak tracked it to a metal bin that clanked in the corner, helpless on its side in a murky pool of rain.

Something brushed against his shoulder.

Varjak gasped, ducked, swung around. What was it? No one there. Just a rustling sound. A plastic bag, caught by the wind, was circling him as if it was the hunter and he was the prey.

He let out his breath, told himself not to be so nervous, and turned back to the bin.

The smell of meat wasn't quite so nice close up. It was rancid, rotten: that was why he'd picked it up from so far away. His nose wrinkled. This wasn't how he'd imagined life Outside. If only he could have a bowl of the Gentleman's caviare now! But this was all he deserved.

Varjak moved towards the bin – and the world erupted into violence. Out of the shadows, those perfect hiding places, five fully grown tomcats sprang. Not one of them wore a collar.

Varjak put up his paws to defend himself. They were too fast. In a vicious blur of speed, they slammed him to the ground and pinned him there.

The biggest, a massive, muscly ginger tom, towered over him. It ripped his cheek with claws as sharp and white as lightning. Varjak howled with pain.

'THESE ARE OUR BINS SONNY!' yelled the ginger. 'AND DON'T FORGET IT!'

Varjak wrenched a paw free and lashed back. He caught the ginger full in the face. It didn't budge; didn't even flinch. It just opened its jaws and spat at him. The other cats poured down on him, a deadly rain of claws and teeth. Varjak screamed. It was agony.

'What do you know about the Vanishings?' demanded the ginger. It was as big as the Gentleman's cats.

'What Vanishings?' gasped Varjak.

'Don't pretend.' Claws raked across Varjak's side. Bony paws pummelled his head. He clenched his eyes tight, and curled into a ball. Off in the distance, he could hear a siren wailing.

This was it. This was the end. He was going to die alone in this lifeless concrete place, and no one would ever know. A sense of relief washed through him. He was glad it was over. He didn't want to live any more. He didn't deserve to live, not after he'd let everyone down.

Already it seemed very far away, like it was happening to someone else. His body felt cold and weightless. As if from a great height, through a curtain of pain, he could hear voices talking. He wondered vaguely whose they were.

'Leave him alone, Ginger.' A gravelly voice.

'Well, look who it is! Friend of yours, is he, Holly?'

'Leave him. He doesn't know anything.'
'Ha! He'll learn.'

Something crunched into Varjak's ribs. Purple pain seared through his body—

. . . and faded into black.

Chapter Fourteen

Down in the darkness, Varjak dreamed.

He was walking by the river in Mesopotamia.

Date palms swayed in the warm breeze. The night air smelled of cinnamon. Jalal walked beside him.

'Jalal! I thought I'd never see you again—'

'Why cinnamon?' said Jalal, as if he hadn't heard. 'Cinnamon?'

'Perhaps you have noticed the smell, all around us? Now follow me and be silent.'

Jalal led him down the river bank towards a group of men. They were sitting around a camp fire, cooking food in a sizzling pan. The most wonderful smell in the world came out of that pan. It was toasty

warm and cinnamonny, and it drove Varjak wild. His nostrils twitched. His mouth drooled. He was starving.

A couple of fat, sluggish cats circled the fire. One of the men tossed them something from the pan. Varjak beamed at Jalal. Obviously they were going to join them. He was going to get some of that delicious-smelling food.

Jalal shook his head. 'Those are not true cats. They have forgotten how to hunt. They are scavengers, trapped here by their own greed. They have become slaves to the people. They might as well be dead already.'

Varjak blushed with shame, remembering that scrap of rancid meat he'd wanted so badly in the city. 'But what if you're hungry and there's nothing else?' he said.

Jalal's eyes blazed amber like the rising sun. 'A cat is an idea of freedom made flesh,' he said fiercely. 'It cannot be tied down. To be truly alive it must be free, and a free cat hunts. It never scavenges or depends on the kindness of people. It depends only on itself.'

Varjak looked down at the ground. He wished it would swallow him up. 'I've failed, Jalal. I've failed you. I've failed everyone.'

'It is no failure to make a mistake, my son. What matters is whether you can learn from it.'

Varjak looked up. The old cat was smiling at him. It was like a ray of sunlight in the night.

'I want to learn how to hunt, Jalal.'

'Then learn you shall. I will restore the knowledge that has been lost. I will teach you Hunting, for it is the Third Skill. Now, show me your Awareness: track down that chirping noise you heard when last you were here.'

Varjak pricked up his ears, determined not to fail again. The noise came from the river bank. With his sensitive whiskers, he probed the air currents that carried the sound until he'd pinned down its source precisely.

'Crickets,' he said. 'Four. Hidden behind that clump of reeds.'

'Correct.' Jalal glided towards the reeds. Varjak marvelled at the way he moved. He was stealth itself. 'When you stalk your prey,' whispered Jalal, 'you become your prey. You make it a part of yourself. Breathe like it breathes. Think like it thinks. When you and the prey are one, you will know its every movement – and then, you will move first. This is the secret of the Third Skill and why it is done best alone. Try it.'

The crickets chirped on behind the long reeds as Varjak and Jalal crept up to them. Varjak selected his target. He sat stock still, waiting, watching, letting all his Awareness flow into the cricket. Every time it shifted, his senses went with it, tracking its speed, trajectory, vectors. He took it all in, as if there was nothing else in the world, as if even he didn't exist any more.

The crickets stirred; they sensed they were being watched. They were about to move – Varjak knew it with absolute certainty.

His legs tensed like steel springs, tight, tight, until the right moment came. He uncoiled into the air. Claws slid out smoothly, pinning the prey, forcing it down to the ground. He opened his jaws, prepared to sink his teeth—

'ENOUGH! ENOUGH!' Jalal was shouting. Varjak released the stunned cricket. What had he done wrong now?

Jalal took a deep breath. 'It was a splendid attack; you have the Third Skill. But this is only practice. You were going to kill it.'

'It's just a cricket!'

'And we are just cats. Remember: you may cause harm only when there is no alternative, only when your life is at stake. You take enough, and no more. That is the way the world is made.'

'I'm sorry, Jalal,' said Varjak, tail between his legs. 'I didn't know.'

'And why did you settle for one cricket? It wouldn't feed a mouse.'

'No one could catch more than one at a time.'

'Oh no?' Jalal grinned. Varjak looked down at his ancestor's paws. The other three crickets were right there, wriggling on the ground.

'Now pay attention,' said Jalal. 'This is how it is done.'

Chapter Fifteen

A tongue the texture of gravel licked Varjak's face, calling him up from the dream.

It scraped a tender spot on his cheek. Blinding colours burst out in his head. He opened his eyes a crack. A black-and-white blur swam into view.

'Hold still,' commanded a gravelly voice. 'I know it hurts, but it has to be done.' Varjak closed his eyes and thought of Mesopotamia, of Jalal, of that delicious cinnamon food he hadn't eaten. Anything, even hunger, was better than this pain.

'There,' she said at last. 'You'll never win a cat show, but you'll live. You'd better live.'

Varjak opened his eyes again. Holly stood above him, Tam behind her.

They were in a narrow, cobbled alleyway, a quiet path along the backs of city buildings. Iron fire escapes led up to sooty windows, far above. Drainpipes snaked down, through grilles in the ground, to sewers below. Varjak thought he could see something glimmering, moving about beneath the streets – but it was night in the alley and he couldn't be sure.

In the distance, he could hear those fearsome metal monsters roaring along the roads. He could taste their poison smoke in the air. He could hear, too, the hisses and growls of street cats as they went about their business. But in this alley the three of them were alone. There was no sign of the ginger tom who had nearly killed him.

He stretched out. Cold, wet cobblestones dug

into his ribs. His body was a pulp of pain. Yet strangely, he didn't feel too bad inside. He was glad he was still alive; glad this cat with the gravelly voice had rescued him.

'You all right, Varjak?' said Holly. 'You've been out for ages.'

'I thought you didn't want friends,' he said.

'We're not friends,' she snapped. 'Tam just made me feel bad about leaving you.'

'Me?' laughed Tam. 'As if I could make her do anything.'

'Anyway, Ginger's gang went too far,' said Holly.

Varjak stood up, unsteadily. 'You stopped them, didn't you? I think you saved my life.'

'All right, all right.' Holly sounded embarrassed; she wouldn't look him in the eye. With one leap, she pounced onto a brick ledge high on the wall, and started to stalk away, spiky as ever.

Varjak wasn't about to lose her again. Without a second thought, he went after her. One moment he was down on the cobbles, the next he was on the ledge. His body seemed to know what to do: he only had to follow Holly. Tam came behind him.

He padded between them to the edge of the wall, where Holly stopped to look up at the sky. Varjak followed her gaze. A white wedge of moon glimmered there. It had grown since he last saw it: it was changing, becoming bigger and brighter.

Varjak looked down from the sky. 'Where are we, exactly?'

'We're in the centre of the city,' said Holly. 'No one else knows about these alleys. You're safe here.'

'Safe from what?'

'From the gangs, stupid. On this side of the park, only the centre is neutral ground. Ginger's gang runs the East. Sally Bones is Boss of the West. Whatever you do, don't try and fight her like you did with Ginger. I don't think anyone could help you if you did that. Ginger's rough, but deep down he's still one of us. Sally Bones – she's something else.'

'Ssh!' hissed Tam. 'She'll hear you!'

'Don't be stupid,' said Holly.

'She's everywhere,' whispered Tam.

'No one's everywhere. It doesn't make sense.'

'Then how else do you explain it?' said Tam. 'You said it yourself – she's not one of us. She's something else.'

Varjak wondered what she meant. 'Not one of us' – that was what his own family used to tell him. 'What's so bad about that?' he said.

Tam's eyes widened as she spoke. '*She's . . . all . . . white.*'

Holly snorted. 'Big deal. You're all brown. So what?'

'She can do things no cat can do,' said Tam darkly.

114

'What sort of things?' said Varjak.

Tam shuddered. 'It's dangerous to even think about it!'

Holly rolled her eyes. Varjak smiled. Tam was always so dramatic.

'I won't tell anyone,' he promised. 'I can keep a secret.'

'Well—' Tam glanced around nervously. 'All right. One thing. She can become invisible. She'll just appear out of thin air, and you don't see her coming till it's too late. That's why no one can beat her in a fight.'

'That's just tales,' said Holly, 'and I don't believe them. But she's the toughest cat in the city, no question. Even Ginger fears Sally Bones—'

'Please!' begged Tam. 'Don't say her name!'

'Her gang's cornering all the food, too,' continued Holly. 'Which is why we need to keep these places secret.' She jumped down from the wall. Varjak and Tam followed her. They shimmied under a low, iron railing into another alley. It would have kept him out if he hadn't seen Holly sneak through first.

'They're moving in on Ginger's turf now. That's why he was so rough when you went for his bins,' she said.

'Which reminds me,' said Tam. 'What are we eating? I'm hungry.'

'Me too,' said Varjak.

Holly shrugged. 'There's nothing here, I've checked already. We could search the park. Or we could go hunting.'

'Hunting means splitting up and going it alone,' said Tam. 'I want to do something all together.' She looked down. 'Besides, hunting's difficult,' she muttered.

'It's not so hard,' said Varjak.

'You?' said Holly, squaring up to him. 'You know how to hunt?'

He wasn't sure. He felt like he did, but he'd only ever hunted in a dream. 'I think so.'

Holly laughed. 'You either can or you can't. And I've never met a pet who could.' She stared at Tam. 'Plenty of street cats can't.'

'Just because you know a lot,' said Tam, 'doesn't mean you're great. I'd rather everyone loved me than be some boring know-it-all.'

'But I do love you, Tam,' grinned Holly. Her mustard eyes sparkled with mischief.

'You do?' said Tam suspiciously.

'Of course I do.' Holly sounded very sincere. Tam relaxed and smiled. 'Everyone does,' continued Holly. Tam's smile grew wider. 'And you know who loves you most of all?'

'Who?' said Tam. 'Who, Holly? Tell me, who?'

'SALLY BONES!' shouted Holly.

Tam leaped back, startled. Holly laughed at the shocked expression on her face. Varjak chuckled. Behind her mustard eyes, Holly had a sense of humour. But poor Tam hadn't seen it coming, and her shaggy brown coat was standing on end.

'That's not very funny,' said Tam as her fur slowly settled.

'Come on,' smiled Holly. 'Let's see what we can find in the park.'

Chapter Sixteen

They emerged from Holly's secret alleys into a back
street. The city was louder here. Varjak could hear
the shrieks and roars of those metal monsters close
by. There were people too; their long, striding
shadows flickered on the walls and their shoes click-
clacked on the pavement.

'Keep your head down,' said Holly as she led the
way through black, rain-soaked streets. 'Don't get
seen. You can't be too careful in this part of town.'

'This is where a lot of Vanishings happened,'
added Tam.

That word again: Vanishings. Everyone seemed
to be talking about it. 'What's a Vanishing?' said
Varjak.

'It happens all over the city,' Tam whispered, 'but
especially here. One day, a cat's there. The next,
they're gone. With no trace, nothing: just gone.
Vanished.' Her brown eyes closed in dread. 'Some
say it's *her*.'

Varjak smiled and looked at Holly, expecting that she'd make a joke of it. But even Holly's tail swished anxiously.

'The truth is, no one knows,' she said, black-and-white fur prickling. 'It's another reason why Ginger and his gang are so edgy right now. They've lost a lot of good cats. Who's next? That's the question.'

The question made Varjak think about home. Who'd be next for the Gentleman and his cats now the Elder Paw was gone? He shivered at the thought. The world he came from and this world Outside were so different. The Gentleman and the Blues meant nothing here; the Contessa's house had no gangs or Vanishings. Was he all that connected the two worlds? So who was he? And where did he belong?

He couldn't go home without a dog, that much he knew. What would it take to make a new life Outside?

'Maybe I should be in a gang,' mused Varjak. In a gang, it wouldn't matter that he wasn't a proper Mesopotamian Blue or that he'd failed his family. No one would know; no one would care. He could be himself, he could be part of something, he could even have friends.

'Gangs are always pushing you around, telling you what to do,' said Holly. 'It's nothing but "Yes Boss" this and "Yes Boss" that.'

'My gang would be different,' said Varjak. 'You could do what you liked in my gang.'

'And who's going to be in this gang with you?'

'Well, there's you two. And me. That's a start.'

'Sounds fun,' said Tam.

Holly laughed. 'You think so? And what about the small problem that one of our gang doesn't have a clue what he's doing?'

Varjak stopped and stood up straight. 'There were five of them!' he protested.

'I don't mean that. I mean – well, everything; everything you need to know to survive in the city. How to find food and shelter. How to stay out of trouble. How to—'

'I can find food. I'm a hunter.' He knew she didn't believe him, but he couldn't stop now. 'I'm the greatest hunter in the world!'

'The greatest hunter in the world?' she scoffed. 'You? Pet cat Varjak? You couldn't even get your own breakfast—'

But Varjak wasn't listening any more. Stung by Holly's words, he followed his senses down a turning off the street. He was going to show her.

'Why are you so mean to him?' said Tam. 'It's obvious he can't hunt, but there's no need—'

'I haven't finished yet! Hey, Varjak, come back! You're not safe on your own! Where are you going?'

'To get my own breakfast,' he growled.

He could hear the buzz of streetlights, the roaring of dogs, the rumbling of the city that never stopped. But above all this he could sense something else; something close, drawing him on.

He followed it into the shadows, further from the lights.

'Come back here!' shouted Holly.

His eyes slowly adjusted to the dark. Deep down the alleyway he glimpsed a soggy mound of paper and boxes. He could smell food: salty, fishy, oily. But that wasn't what had drawn him. His Awareness started to tingle. There was something else . . .

It was as if he was being watched – not just by Holly and Tam, but by some part of the darkness, with eyes as black as shadow. He let his Awareness flow out. What he sensed was odd and cold: something not quite alive, but not quite dead either. He frowned. It felt wrong.

'Varjak Paw! It's dangerous down there! Come back right now!' It was Holly. He turned, hushed her, and turned back, the tension rising within him. But that strange sensation was gone, leaving no trace. Had he just imagined it? All this talk of Vanishings was getting to him . . .

Puzzled, he probed the shadows again with his whiskers. Motion. This time he felt motion, out there in the dark. What was it? Hidden behind the rubbish, something small and sleek was moving—

A mouse. It was only a mouse.

He let out the tension, and grinned. That must have been it all along. Nothing more than a real, live, and very breakfast-sized mouse.

So this is it, he told himself. Your big moment. Your first prey. This is not a toy. This is not a dream. It's real, and it's happening now.

Don't move, not till it's in range. Don't even breathe. Here . . . here it comes. It thinks it's safe.

Hunting, the Third Skill: *When you stalk your prey, you become your prey.*

Varjak's senses went out to it, tracing its tiniest movements, merging with it in his mind. The mouse came closer . . . closer . . .

CRACK! His paws shot out, slapped the mouse's head, hard. Stunned it. Held it down. Jaws closed around its neck. Teeth sank in: the lethal bite.

Varjak gasped. He had killed for real. And it was like killing a part of himself.

I'm sorry, he thought, beginning to shake. I'm sorry. But I have to eat.

Enough and no more. That is the way the world is made.

He stooped and gently picked up the body. His first kill. He gave silent thanks, and crunched into his breakfast.

It was strange. On the outside, it looked and even smelled like that toy mouse back in the Contessa's house. But as soon as he bit into it, he knew this was something new. It tasted so different to anything he'd eaten before. Real food, fresh and warm. It satisfied him completely.

'Did you see that?' said Tam. 'Did you see the way he did it, Holly? *Bam!* It never had a chance!'

'I saw it,' said Holly.

'Wasn't it something?' beamed Tam. 'Where did you learn to do that, Varjak? Will you teach me?'

'Actually,' he admitted, 'that was the first time.'

Holly nodded. 'I thought it might be. Still, I've seen worse. A lot worse.' She winked. 'Maybe you're not as useless as you look, Mr Paw.'

Varjak smiled. He'd never have to rely on people again. He was a hunter now. He had the Third Skill.

Tam's nostrils twitched. 'What's that smell?' she said. Varjak and Holly sniffed the air. The alley curved away into complete darkness, and that salty, fishy tang was coming from a place they couldn't see, further down. The scent reminded Varjak of the Gentleman's caviare – another thing he'd never have to eat.

'It smells great,' said Tam. 'I'm going after it.'

'I wouldn't,' warned Holly. 'We're too near Ginger's turf. You don't want to risk it. Wait for the park.'

Tam licked her chops. 'At least it's not *her* territory. And it smells so good, Holly. There's no one else around, it'll be OK. Come on, Varjak, let's eat!'

'You really like that smell?' he said.

'It's already dangerous here,' said Holly. 'I'm not going any further.'

'You killjoy,' muttered Tam. 'Holly knows best. Holly always knows best.'

'It's true. I do.'

'Well, I bet there's nothing to eat in the park,' said Tam. 'So there.'

She was right. The park had been picked clean already. They could find no food at all. They came away hungry – except for Varjak Paw.

Chapter Seventeen

In his dreams that night, Varjak was back in Mesopotamia. The date palms swayed in the warm breeze, and the cinnamon smell of cooking filled the air. He looked down at the river, where the moon and stars glimmered, so big and bright he could almost bite them.

'This river is called the Tigris,' said Jalal. 'One day I will show you more of the Tigris, for it can teach you much. But tonight, we must practise the Fourth Skill: Slow-Time.'

The old cat seemed to shimmer for a moment.

Varjak blinked, and the shimmering stopped. 'What was that?'

'Slow-Time,' said Jalal. 'I can move faster than you can see.'

Varjak's eyes widened. Slow-Time was a skill the Elder Paw had talked of. Slow-Time, Moving Circles, Shadow-Walking. 'Teach me, Jalal.'

'Slow-Time begins with breathing,' explained his ancestor. 'So first of all, you must learn to breathe. Count your breaths. In, out, in, out. You see? You breathe fast and shallow, like most cats. Breathe more deeply. Yes. Use the whole of your lungs. Good. Now count. In–two–three, out–two–three. In–two–three, out–two–three.'

They sat by the rippling Tigris, breathing slower and slower.

'Slower,' said Jalal. 'In–two–three–four, out–two–three–four. Very good. Slow the stream of your thoughts. Once you are in Slow-Time, everything will seem to slow down around you. But you will be fast. You will be faster than anything.'

Varjak looked up at the Mesopotamian sky. He could see the starlight bending across vast distances of space and time. A strange energy pulsed through him. His body felt light, light like light itself.

'The slower you go, the faster you are,' said Jalal. 'You feel it? You s-l-o-w yourself down.' The energy throbbed in Varjak's belly. Jalal's voice sounded like it was stretching, melting, radiating in every direction. 'Do not be alarmed. This is Slow-Time. Now practise the Skill!'

Chapter Eighteen

'I'm starving,' grumbled Tam, late the next night, back in their alleys. The three of them sat on a high brick wall together, thinking about food. 'My belly's shrinking. I can feel it.'

'Me too,' said Varjak. 'That mouse was good, but it was only a mouse.'

'You're right,' said Holly. 'This is getting serious. It's time for drastic action, and I've got a plan.' She looked Varjak up and down. 'First of all, though, you've got to look normal. Tell me, Mr Paw, are you ever planning to clean yourself?'

Varjak shook his head. He was Outside; he didn't have to wash. 'At home, Mother was always washing me. I hated it.'

'You're not at home now.'

'Here she goes,' sighed Tam.

'I don't have to do anything I don't like,' said Varjak.

'You can do what you want,' agreed Holly, 'but

look at you! The people will notice. They'll think you're wild and they'll take you away.'

Varjak inspected his coat. She was right: he was filthy. The fine silver-blue fur was completely caked with grime.

'I like it,' he said, rather pleased with himself.

'Plus,' she added, 'you stink.' He didn't respond. 'I'm sorry, but you really do.' Varjak looked to Tam, but even she was silent this time.

'OK, OK,' he grumbled, reluctantly licking his paws. 'You sound just like Mother sometimes.' He stopped after a few licks. 'Is that better?'

Holly looked him calmly in the eye. 'I'm not saying this to annoy you. I'm saying it because it's dangerous to look so dirty. You'll draw attention to us all, and you'll ruin my plan. Now do it properly or I'm off.' Varjak snorted, but resumed his cleaning. 'If you're a Blue whatever-it-is, you should be proud of how you look,' she coaxed.

'We are the noblest of cats,' he muttered through a mouthful of mud. But the old boast rang hollow in the city. Would any of his family rescue a stranger? The Elder Paw, perhaps; not the rest. So who was more noble: the Blue, or this spiky street cat who'd saved his life?

The question bothered him. It turned everything he believed on its head. So he pushed it out of his mind and concentrated on his cleaning.

'All right,' said Holly at last. 'That'll do.' Varjak's fur was a dull grey colour. It looked very ordinary. It didn't look like the coat of a Mesopotamian Blue any more – and he liked it that way.

'Now the collar,' she said. 'You can't be a street cat with a collar. Come here.'

This was more like it. He'd always hated that thing around his neck. Holly gnawed at the collar. He was vulnerable, balanced on top of a wall, with her sharp teeth just a bite away from his throat. But he trusted Holly. She'd rescued him. She was his friend.

'There.' She moved back. Varjak wiggled his shoulders, and the hated collar fluttered down. It fell through the bars of a metal grille, and disappeared into the sewers beneath the city. Now he was just another street cat with no ties, no family, and no home.

'Good,' said Holly. 'You're one of us. If we run into them, that's what you say.'

'Run into who?' said Varjak, though he knew the answer already. He grinned. 'Not that big, bad, Sal—'

'Please!' cried Tam. 'You don't know what you're saying!'

'This isn't a joke,' said Holly. She sounded serious. Varjak stopped grinning. 'We have to pass near her territory to get where we're going. Remember what Ginger did to you? These cats are worse. *Much* worse.'

They set off silently, each in their own thoughts. Holly led them through the back streets, always taking the ways that were quiet and hidden. But the light and noise grew stronger the further they went. The rumbling of the city was louder, harsher. Soon they couldn't avoid the dirty orange glare of street lights. They were in the open now, coming up to a crossroads.

Holly's fur prickled up fast. 'Hide!' she hissed.

They pressed themselves back into the alley, just in time to see a column of cats patrolling the other side of the crossroads. Varjak's insides knotted as he saw them, and his cheek burned where Ginger had slashed him. Holly was right. They looked much worse than the cat who'd nearly killed him.

There were seven of them. They swaggered and strutted on the sidewalk as if they owned the whole world. Other cats got out of their way, scurrying aside as they approached. At the head of the column was a brawny tom with stripy fur. Varjak caught a glimpse of his face. It was covered in scars.

'That's Razor,' whispered Tam. 'One of *her* lieutenants.'

The three of them crouched silently in their hiding place, watching, waiting, until the patrol had passed.

'OK,' said Holly at last. 'It's clear now. Let's move before they come back.'

'This crossroads is the boundary,' Tam told Varjak as they left the safety of the alley. 'Don't ever cross it.'

'I won't,' he said.

There were no shadowy alleys where Holly took them. Instead, there were tall, white buildings arranged in a square. In its centre was a water fountain, and a huge stone column pointing up at the sky.

Around the column's base there were four statues, one at each corner. They were statues of lions, made of gleaming bronze. They were giants. Each paw was the size of a man. They had shaggy, wild manes around their heads; proud, free, fearless faces.

They were so powerful, so magnificent, so sure of themselves.

'That's what we should be,' whispered Tam.

'What we *could* be,' said Varjak. 'They're great.'

They sat there for a while, just looking at the statues.

'We can only come here late at night,' said Holly. 'During the day it's too crowded: people, cars, dogs. But at least it's neutral ground; the gangs leave it alone. Which means they also leave those birds alone.'

Varjak looked again. He was so thrilled by the statues, he'd hardly noticed that the square was

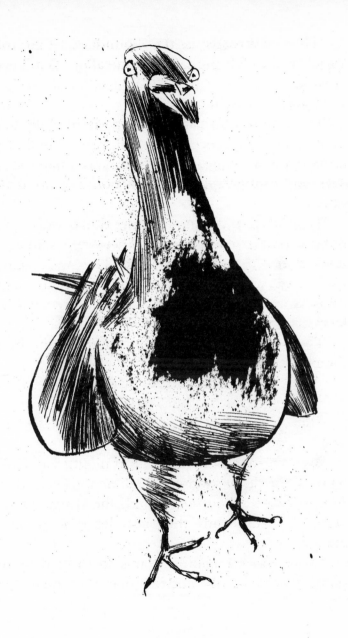

swarming with pigeons. Dozens of them strutted about beneath the moonlight, and more were coming in all the time. The air pulsed with their trilling and cooing.

'So tell me, Mr Paw,' said Holly. 'How exactly would you hunt one?'

'What do you mean?' said Varjak, suddenly suspicious. Was she making fun of him again? He'd never tried to hunt a bird; it seemed too difficult.

'I mean, go and get one of those pigeons.'

It sounded like a challenge. He searched her mustard eyes. She didn't look like she was making

fun of him. She meant it.

'All right,' he said. 'I will.'

'Holly!' said Tam. 'That's not fair. Don't take any notice of her, Varjak. She's being mean again.'

'I want to do it,' he said, still looking into Holly's eyes. She smiled.

Varjak slunk into the square. He selected a bird and turned all his Awareness onto it. He observed it with his eyes, ears, whiskers. Nothing it did could surprise him now: he and it were one.

He crept towards the pigeon, stealthy as Jalal himself. In the whole world, there was nothing but him and his prey. Varjak sprang –

– and a hundred wings came at him; a hundred claws curved out; a hundred beaks cawed in chaos.

Panic! Varjak fled from the flock. He hadn't expected anything so fierce. His fur ruffled and his tail trembled. He hid behind Holly and Tam, and watched the birds settle down from a safe distance.

'Varjak!' cried Tam. 'Are you OK?' He shook his head. 'I told you, Holly, no one could do that!'

'Exactly,' said Holly. 'That's exactly what happens to me every time. That's why even the gangs don't bother with this place. But I always think, if we could just work out how to catch the birds, we'd never go

hungry again.'

'It's impossible,' panted Varjak. His pulse was still pounding. 'Impossible!'

'For one cat, yes,' said Holly. 'And yes, we usually hunt alone. But imagine three of us –'

'– hunting together –'

'– it could just work. Well, that's the plan. What do you think?'

'Yes,' said Varjak Paw.

'I don't like the sound of this,' said Tam. She buried her head in her paws, and curled up to sleep. 'Wake me up when it's time to go home.'

Chapter Nineteen

Varjak and Holly talked through the night by the giant bronze lions. There was nothing to distract them but the fountain's trickle and the birds' trilling.

It was strange at first. No one else had ever wanted to talk about hunting before. Varjak could still barely believe that someone his own age was interested in it, and not senseless kitten games like Jay, Jethro and Jerome. But it was true. Holly was easy to talk to because she was like him. She liked the same things. Her mind worked in the same way.

Sometimes it was hard to keep up with her. Whenever he thought he had the answer to something, she asked another difficult question: why like this, not like that? And she had ideas he would never have thought up. But he had a few of his own, too; and together they worked out their plan.

That night, Varjak felt something he'd never felt

before. Or rather, he didn't feel something. He didn't feel alone any more.

They woke Tam just before dawn and explained the plan to her. Her eyes grew round with fear.

'Me?' she said. 'You want *me* to do *that*? Why me?'

'Can you do my part of the plan?' said Holly. 'Or Varjak's?'

'Well, no – but—'

'You've got to do it, Tam,' said Varjak. 'It's impossible without you.'

'It is?' she said.

'Of course it is,' said Holly. 'And if you do it, I promise I won't say *her* name any more.'

'Well then,' said Tam cheerfully, 'what are we waiting for?'

They took up their positions as the first rays of sunshine splashed onto the white buildings, filling the square with light. Everything began to glow: the ground, the sky, even the water in the fountain. Varjak crept up on the pigeons from one corner of the square. Holly crept up from another. Tam stood in front of them, on the far side of the flock.

At Holly's signal, Tam sprang at the pigeons. A hundred birds beat their wings, fierce and dangerous in their flock. Tam kept going, never slowing, just aiming for the other side in a blur of speed they couldn't stop – and Varjak and Holly flew out of the morning sun behind them.

It should have been easy. The birds were distracted by Tam and didn't see them coming in the haze of brilliant light. That was the plan.

But even as Varjak dived in, the thrill of the hunt in his veins, it started to go wrong. Tam was clear through, but there were still too many pigeons in a mass. He and Holly were on the edge of the flock, but couldn't get close enough to any single bird to strike.

The birds turned on Holly, wings flapping savagely, claws curving out. She didn't run. She stood there bravely, trying hard, but now they were surrounding her, pecking at her with shrill, sharp beaks.

Holly was in trouble. She was trapped and she couldn't get out. They were tearing, scratching, ripping at her. Varjak could see panic mounting in her face. Tam was helpless on the other side. Quick – he had to do something quick!

Slow-Time, the Fourth Skill: *everything will seem to slow down around you. But you will be fast. You will be faster than anything.*

Would it work in the real world? He breathed in–two–three–four. Out–two–three–four.

And the wings . . . slowed . . . down.

Varjak could see each beat, each claw, as if in slow motion. He dived after Holly into the mass of birds, moving smoothly through the chaos, making them fly apart for just a moment.

'Holly!' he called. She looked up. It was enough to break the rising terror in her eyes. She darted through the gap he'd made, away from the flock and towards Tam, to safety.

Out of danger now, Varjak breathed normally – and switched out of Slow-Time. It worked! The Fourth Skill really worked!

'Did they hurt you?' he panted as he caught up with her.

'Nothing wrong with me,' said Holly, though she was trembling. 'Thanks for getting me out,' she added, much more quietly.

'No problem.'

'He saved you, Holly!' bubbled Tam.

'I guess we're even now,' she muttered.

'I didn't do it for that,' said Varjak.

Holly didn't meet his eyes, but just for a second, Varjak thought he saw a smile flicker on her face. 'Come on,' she said, sidling away from the square. 'We've got to hurry. I don't want to be here in broad daylight. It's too dangerous.'

'You don't want another go?' said Varjak. He knew she was shaken – her fur was still ruffled – but maybe it would help to try again.

'Why bother?' she said, padding back through the city. 'The plan didn't work. It was a stupid idea.'

'No, it wasn't,' said Varjak, keeping pace with her, ahead of Tam. 'And you did everything you could—'

'How about me?' said Tam. 'Did I do all right, Varjak?'

'You were great. You were both really brave.'

'I was great,' beamed Tam.

'There were just too many of them, this time,' said Varjak. 'But that doesn't mean it's impossible.'

'Maybe,' said Holly, picking up the pace. 'Maybe if we tried it another way—'

They started on a new plan as they headed back. The city was beginning to rumble with life once more. Familiar streets flashed past as they went by.

'I'm still hungry,' said Tam. Her nostrils twitched. 'Wait, you two! It's that fishy smell again.' She stopped by a turning off a side street, the same turning where Varjak had caught the mouse. Even in daylight it curved away into darkness, into shadow.

'Come on, Tam,' said Holly, over her shoulder.

'But it's that lovely smell again,' said Tam. 'And there wasn't any food in the park, and the hunting didn't work, and I'm still hungry.'

'We're not stopping here,' said Holly. 'If you go, you're on your own.' She turned back to Varjak, and carried on talking. They walked away, planning their next hunt together. Tam stayed behind at the turning.

'It's your loss,' called Tam. 'I'll see you back in our alleys.'

Chapter Twenty

Tam didn't return that day.

At first, Holly laughed it off – 'She's probably still stuffing her face!' – but when Tam didn't show up by nightfall, or the next morning either, she began to look worried.

'It was the same street where you caught the mouse, wasn't it?' said Holly. 'I had a bad feeling about that place.'

Varjak thought back to that strange sensation he'd had in the turning. Maybe there was something else out there, after all. 'You know, I had a bad feeling too.'

'Let's go and find her,' said Holly, as the rain began to fall.

They started in the very place where Tam left them. They followed the turning she'd gone down, into the shadows, but it just led out onto another alleyway. There was no sign of Tam. Nothing: not even with Varjak's Awareness. It was just an ordinary street.

They ranged wider, across the centre of the city, where the street cats who weren't in either of the gangs lived. None of them had seen Tam.

They tried Ginger's territory next. Near the concrete blocks where Holly had saved Varjak, they found some cats from Ginger's gang, sheltering from the rain.

'I'm looking for Tam,' said Holly. 'Any of you seen her?' They said they hadn't.

'Do you believe them?' asked Varjak, as they headed for the park.

'Ginger's gang are rough but they're honest,' said Holly. 'If Tam ran into them, if there'd been any trouble, they'd tell us.'

Tam wasn't in the park either. They searched till twilight. They found a few scraps of food, but not a sign of Tam among the wet, dead leaves.

Tired and soaked from the hard rain that fell through the day, they headed back to Holly's alleys. On their way, they met a big stripy tom, prowling in a covered, cobbled passage. Varjak recognized him at once by the slash marks on his face. He didn't look friendly – Varjak's dripping fur prickled at the sight of him – but he smiled at Holly, showing a set of sharp white teeth.

'Razor,' said Holly.

'Holly,' nodded the stripy tom. 'Good to see you. Where's that shaggy cat you're always with?'

'Tam. She's – I don't know where she is. Have you seen her?'

Razor shook his head. 'No. But she hasn't been near Sally Bones's territory, I'm sure of that.'

'How do you know?'

'It's my job.' He licked his paws proudly. 'Who's this you've got with you?' He flicked his tail in Varjak's direction, but didn't look at him, as if he wasn't worth wasting time over.

'I'm Varjak Paw,' said Varjak.

The tom's tail twitched with contempt. 'I wasn't talking to you,' he said. Varjak fell silent.

'Nothing to worry about,' said Holly quickly. 'He's one of us. Just a pet who got lost.'

Razor sniffed. 'Why waste your time with a pet? Come and join our gang. You know Sally Bones'll win in the end. This city's hers.'

Holly smiled, but didn't say anything.

'You'll be safe from the Vanishings,' said Razor. 'Sally looks after her own.'

'Thank you, Razor,' said Holly, 'but you know I've never wanted to be in a gang, and I've got to look for Tam now.' She began to move away. Razor stepped in front of her, muscles rippling.

'Come on, Holly,' he said. 'I've always liked you.' Holly was still smiling, but Varjak could see her trying to edge away. 'You could be somebody, in a gang,' said Razor, moving closer, following

her. 'You could be important. I could make you important.'

'I don't want—'

'Come on,' insisted Razor. 'I'll take you to meet the Boss. I'm one of her top cats now.' There was a flash of fear in Holly's mustard eyes. Varjak saw it.

'She told you, she doesn't want to,' he said, without thinking.

Razor turned to him. The scars on his face writhed like snakes.

'I warned you already,' he growled.

SLAM!

A rock-hard paw smashed into Varjak's face. Varjak reeled, stunned, and sank to the ground in a pool of rain. He wanted to get up, to fight back, but his legs were like soggy paper and the world was spinning around him.

'Don't get in my way again,' snarled Razor. His words twirled above Varjak's head like stars. One hit. That was all it took. And he didn't even see it coming.

The brawny tom turned back to Holly. 'When you've had enough of wasting your time with weak little losers, and you want to see what it's like being a real cat – come and find me.'

He padded away, tail held high.

'Varjak?' said Holly, when he was gone. 'Are you all right?'

Varjak shook his head. Blood trickled out of his mouth. He wiped it away with the back of his paw. It matted on his fur.

'It was brave, standing up to him,' she said, 'but it was stupid. You can't win a fight with Razor.'

'I'll beat him one day,' said Varjak.

'You're crazy,' she sighed. 'You've got to learn to use your brain. There's no point fighting cats like that. The best you can do is keep out of their way.'

'I will beat him,' Varjak vowed. Whoever had left those scars on Razor's face had managed it. He could do it too.

'You're not going to beat anyone today, Mr Paw,' said Holly. 'Come on. Let's keep looking for Tam.'

Chapter Twenty-one

Varjak's wounds healed as the moon grew bigger in the sky. He slept most days in Holly's alleys, or hunted and foraged for food with her. By night, they searched the city for Tam. He was worried about her, but he liked learning about hidden ways and secret paths that no one else knew.

Together, he and Holly walked the city's walls, its window-ledges, its shadowy back streets. They always kept clear of people, though they could often hear them close by. They stayed away from the wide main roads; and they never approached or even mentioned those shrieking, roaring metal monsters that prowled up and down them.

Everywhere they went they asked about Tam. No one had seen her. Neither Varjak nor Holly said the word aloud, but it was beginning to look like Tam had Vanished.

'Now,' said Holly, 'there's one part of the city we haven't searched yet, and it's time we did.'

'Sally Bones's territory?'

'It's dangerous – but we've got to try it.'

Varjak didn't say anything. He didn't think they'd find Tam there – they were nowhere near it the last time they saw her – and he didn't want to run into Razor again so soon. But he was curious about the tales of Sally Bones, the cat who was white and could appear out of thin air.

Holly led the way through the streets, out of their familiar ground and into parts of the city Varjak hadn't been in before, though he'd glimpsed them from the hill long ago.

The streets became bigger the further they went. So did the buildings. One of them was almost high as a hill, and its outline sparkled with lights. It had a glass front: windows instead of walls. Each showed something different inside.

Varjak peered into a window. There were animals in there, ranged out and displayed on glass shelves. Little furry mice, fluffy rabbits, colourful birds. Their eyes were open, but they were silent and still. It was as if they were stuck in the moment, frozen in time, forever about to move but never quite making it.

'Stop staring, Mr Paw,' said Holly. 'Never seen a toy shop before?'

'What are they?'

'The toys? They're nothing. Children play with

153

them.' She moved off down the pavement. 'Come on, we can't hang about on Sally Bones's territory.' Varjak tore his eyes away from the frozen scene and followed her, but he was getting the strangest feeling. It was like in the alley, before the mouse hunt. A cold sensation: being watched by something not quite alive, not quite dead.

He let his Awareness flow out again, and found the source. It was coming from a stack of boxes by the toy shop door. One box had fallen on its side and split open. The flap hung loose and limp.

'I am very well thank you please,' said a tinny little voice from inside the box. It rustled, and out came a cat.

Varjak's first thought was that it looked like Tam, or a cruel joke about Tam. It had her shaggy chocolate-brown fur and comfortable look, but everything else was horribly wrong. Like the animals in the window, it didn't seem real. Its eyes were wide open, but they were glassy, expressionless. It was smiling, but the smile was weirdly empty. It talked, but back to front, nonsense.

'Tam?' said Varjak. 'Tam?'

'Happy, happy, happy,' said the cat.

Varjak's fur stood on end. 'It's Tam!' he cried. 'Look, Holly – what's happened to her?'

'Don't be stupid,' said Holly. 'It's a toy.' She peered closer at the cat. Its head nodded, bobbing up and down cheerfully. 'It's a good one, very realistic. Look at the detail – the fur's perfect.'

'But it's Tam's fur—'

'Tam's fur was never so neat.' Holly sniffed it. 'Doesn't smell like a cat, does it? And listen to it. That's not how any cat talks.'

'I be your friend forever!' said the toy, in its strange, hollow voice.

'Oh, Holly, it's horrible . . . I'm sure it's Tam!'

Holly wheeled about and faced him, mustard eyes on fire. 'Of course it's not Tam!' she yelled. 'Get it through your head! Tam's gone, see? She's Vanished.' There was a moment of silence. Even the toy cat seemed to be hanging on her words.

'There, I said it. She's Vanished. She was a greedy idiot, and now she's Vanished, another fine friend who's left me. She's not coming back. Ever. Understand?'

Varjak had never seen her so upset. He knew Holly missed her friend, of course, but she was so spiky and cool, she'd never shown it before. 'Are we going to keep looking for her?' he said softly.

'Here's your pretty kittycat!' said the toy.

Holly closed her eyes. 'No. She's not here. She's not anywhere. She's Vanished.' She shook her head. 'I'm sorry I shouted at you. It's just – that's not Tam.'

Varjak peered again at the toy cat. She was right. Tam had Vanished, but this wasn't her. It looked like her, but that was all. It wasn't even alive. Wasn't even dead.

A cat which was not quite a cat. And behind it, there were more just the same, shuffling around in the broken box.

'I am very well thank you please,' they said.

He shivered. 'I don't like them,' he said. 'Why would anyone want one of those when they could have a real cat?'

'People like toy cats better than real cats,' said Holly. 'No looking after. They do what you want. They're always nice and cute. Not like us.' She grinned. 'Not like you, anyway. You couldn't get a toy cat to stink if you tried.' He had to smile. 'Come on,'

157

she said. 'Let's get out of here before we run into Sally Bones. Let's go home.'

Varjak's mind whirled as they sped back through the city. He didn't like these toy cats, not one bit. But then he remembered that toy mouse, back in the Contessa's house: how real it had seemed, and how much he'd wanted to play with it.

The Contessa's house. He hadn't thought about it often, with all that was happening, but the idea brought pictures to his mind. An empty armchair. An antique fireplace. A row of china bowls. The pictures were hard to hold on to. They kept changing into other pictures. The harder he tried to hold on to them, the harder it became. Even the garden that night: the Gentleman's lips: the way his cats moved – it was all fading.

At that moment, Varjak felt he would give anything to be with his family again. Away in the distance, he heard the muffled roar of a metal monster. A great wave of sadness washed up from his stomach.

'Let's stop here, Mr Paw,' said Holly suddenly, snapping him out of his thoughts. She pointed at a covered alley. 'We're still on Sally's turf, but it's more dangerous to walk through her streets now than to sleep here for the day.' She smiled at him. He tried to smile back. Couldn't. 'Hey, what's wrong?' she said.

'I want to go home.'

'I told you, it's safer to stay here.'

'Not that home. My old home, on the hill.'

'Still thinking about that?' She shrugged. 'What's stopping you?'

'I can't. I was supposed to go back with a dog, to save my family from the Gentleman and his cats. I tried to get one, Holly. I stood there, in front of those monsters, but I just couldn't do it. I couldn't even get them to talk.' He closed his eyes, the shame still stinging like a new-cut wound. 'I failed.'

'It's not your fault,' she said gently. 'Dogs are scary. Stupid, too. I've never heard of a cat who could talk to them.'

Varjak sighed. Jalal could do it, he knew that. But he was no Jalal. He wasn't even a proper Mesopotamian Blue. 'All I know is I've let everyone down. I can never, ever go back. Without a dog, I don't have a home any more.'

'That's not true. The whole world's your home now. Even Sally Bones's territory.' She winked a mustard eye at him. 'Let's get some sleep. It'll seem better tomorrow. You never know what's around the corner.'

They settled down, side by side, in the shadows of the alley. There was no invisible barrier between them any more. There hadn't been for quite a while.

Chapter Twenty-two

Varjak dreamed.

He dreamed he was walking by the Tigris. Zigzag palms swayed in the cinnamon breeze. The sky was vivid with stars.

Jalal walked beside him, shimmering in Slow-Time. Varjak breathed in–two–three–four, and slowed himself down, until he felt the energy pulsing inside him. Only then could he clearly see how Jalal was moving.

It was different to anything he'd ever imagined. All cats are graceful, but Jalal was a river of energy, like the Tigris, flowing and changing itself at will.

'Your body,' said Jalal, 'is but a part of you. You are more than your body. You can make it do anything, if you know how. You can dodge any blow, you can strike any enemy, you can win any fight. I will show you how – for that is the Fifth Skill, and we call it Moving Circles.'

His silver-blue frame started to twist into shapes as strange as those stars above.

First, he made a soft velvet arch of himself. Varjak copied him. He stretched his spine as far as it would go – and then a bit further.

Next, Jalal's arch curved round on itself, became a fluid figure of eight. Varjak followed him, made the move. It was a giant stretch. He felt pain – hot, white pain – but he felt something else as well. The energy that pulsed in his belly was changing into a new kind of power.

And now Jalal's figure of eight melted into a circle, an endless Moving Circle. Varjak breathed in deeply, and followed his ancestor. His whole body shook under the strain. But that power was building up, growing stronger, a warm flow, free and unlimited; a Moving Circle, like Jalal.

It felt like he was glowing.

'Good,' said Jalal. 'Now the last movement. Open the Circle. Let loose the energy, take it outwards. Use your momentum to direct the force. Like this.'

Jalal's paw appeared out of nowhere, a whisker from Varjak's nose. He hadn't seen it coming at all. His eyes widened. If he could master this Skill, he could beat anyone.

'Strike me,' said the old cat.

Varjak breathed, moved, opened his Circle. Jalal arched aside – a moment too late. Varjak skimmed the fur on his shoulder.

A surprised smile appeared on Jalal's face.

'Well,' he said. 'You have travelled far since first we met, Varjak Paw. But remember: you take enough, and no more. No matter how tempting, you may cause harm only when your life is in danger.' His eyes sparkled amber, like sunrise. 'Which it is. Now wake up!'

Chapter Twenty-three

Varjak woke from his dream in the alley.

It was night time again; he and Holly had slept through the day. A street light buzzed on and off behind him. A full moon, round and white as a saucer of milk, shone comfortingly up above, but it was quickly smothered by street-black clouds.

He needed to go to the litter tray. Holly was fast asleep, and they were still on Sally Bones's territory. Well, it was all Outside, wasn't it? The whole world was his litter tray. He could go wherever he pleased.

He slouched out of the shadows and did his business by a heap of rubbish. What a relief it was.

His Awareness tingled. The fur on the back of his neck prickled. It felt like he was being watched. He swivelled to face the top of the alley – and immediately wished he hadn't.

A thin white cat sat there. She was licking her claws, watching him with one ice blue eye. Where the other eye should've been was an empty socket.

Her fur was spotless clean, but around her was the smell of darkness, of dank and deadly things and places.

By her side prowled a dozen street cats, thick-necked and bristling, grimy as the city itself. They were bigger than the white cat, but somehow they looked like soft little kittens beside her.

'Good, was it, sonny?' she asked. Varjak couldn't answer. He kept staring at her, unable to speak. She was all muscle and bone. He could see her ribs. They jutted out as if they were trying to escape from her.

'Now, this isn't your territory,' she said, flexing her bone-white claws. 'And you shouldn't ever do what you've just done all over someone else's territory. Especially if that someone is me.'

She smiled a crooked smile, but her single eye stayed cold and hard. He had no doubt who he was looking at. No wonder poor Tam was terrified of Sally Bones.

'Speak when the Boss talks to you,' growled a stripy tom with slash marks all over his face. Varjak recognized him: Razor.

Holly stood up beside Varjak. 'He didn't mean it,' she said. 'He's new here.' Her legs quivered, but her voice was steady.

'New, is he?' said the thin white cat. Her tail swished angrily. She nodded at the stripy tom. 'Razor. Why wasn't I told about this?'

The tom began to shake. 'I didn't think it was important, Boss. He's just a pet—'

The air seemed to shimmer for a moment – and then Razor howled and clutched his face. There was a fresh, new slash mark across one side. And the white cat's claws were tipped with blood.

'It's not your job to think, Razor,' she hissed. 'It's

your job to tell me everything. And if you can't do your job, I'll find someone else who can. Understand?'

Razor nodded, still clutching his face. In that moment of quiet, Varjak could hear his own heart, thumping in his throat.

'Now get some information out of this new cat,' spat Sally Bones. 'I have a feeling he's something to do with the Vanishings. Luger and Wes: you two watch his little friend.'

Razor and the other two cats came towards Varjak and Holly. Holly's ears twitched nervously.

'Why couldn't you wait till we got home?' she whispered. 'We've had it now.'

'We could make it over those walls,' said Varjak, searching for a way out.

'They'd only catch us. At least Razor's doing it, not her.' Holly shivered. 'Just don't tell them about my alleys, OK?'

Razor marched up to them, eyes slitted, claws glinting. The slash on his face was red and raw.

'What's your name, trouble-maker?' he snarled.

'Varjak Paw.'

'Where are you from?'

'Mesopotamia.'

Razor's scarred face twisted into a scowl. 'Very funny. Where are you really from? Where do you sleep?'

Varjak glanced at Holly. What could he do? Anything he said could give her secret away. He could only keep it by staying silent.

'Are you going to open up?' said Razor. His mouth curled back, baring his teeth. 'Or do I have to open you up?'

There was no sound at all in the alley except the street light's buzz. Varjak kept his mouth shut. They all stared at him: Razor, Sally Bones, her gang: all staring at him. Varjak felt boxed in and alone. The pressure mounted in his head. But he stared straight back at Razor without a word. He was determined not to look away.

'Well?' demanded Razor. The tom's eyes burned into him, but Varjak hung on. Don't look away. Don't let him win. Hang on. Hang on. *Hang on.*

Somewhere in the distance, a monster roared.

Razor blinked and looked away. Varjak relaxed. And in that instant, something slashed his cheek.

Razor's claws. Varjak reeled back, stunned. His head was on fire.

'I'm going to teach you a lesson you'll never forget,' growled Razor. He came forward. Varjak lashed out. The street cat dodged easily, and jabbed his jaw in return. Blood sprayed from Varjak's face in a thick red fountain.

Another hit to the face. Varjak's legs felt weak. Out of the corner of his eye, he saw Holly start to move – but Luger and Wes moved faster, blocking her off. It was just him and Razor.

'Not so tough, are you?' spat Razor. 'I can finish you any time. I'm going easy on you. Now talk!' He slammed Varjak's ribs, knocking him off balance. Varjak staggered into the rubbish heap. It squelched around him. He was still standing, but he couldn't take another hit.

Moving Circles, the Fifth Skill: *You can dodge any blow, you can strike any enemy.* It was his only chance.

Varjak breathed as Razor came up for the kill.

In–two–three–four. Energy pulsed in Varjak's belly. Out–two–three–four. Time slowed down.

In–two–three–four. Razor struck in slow motion. Out–two–three–four. Varjak made a Moving Circle.

In–two–three–four. Razor missed. Out–two–three–four. This is good, thought Varjak Paw.

He could see the others, staring at him. Holly's mouth hung open in surprise.

Razor bared his teeth, came in again, moving as if through mud. Varjak opened his Circle, let loose the energy – and hit Razor with everything he had, right between the eyes.

Chapter Twenty-four

Razor's head jerked back. Varjak had struck his target!

But the big tom was strong. It was only enough to daze him. He stepped out of Varjak's reach, and shook his head, as if he couldn't believe he'd been hit.

'Enough!' Sally Bones shouted. Varjak looked to the top of the alley – but she wasn't there.

'Where did you learn that?' her voice demanded from behind him. He wheeled about. There was the faintest shimmer of white, but she was gone again.

'Who taught you?' she hissed, from somewhere inside his head. And before Varjak knew what was happening, she had him pinned flat on the ground, white bones above him, single blue eye burning into him. He lost the rhythm of his breath – and everything sped up again. He was out of Slow-Time. 'Answer me!' she said. 'Who taught you?'

He couldn't move; he couldn't hide. 'Jalal!' he cried, helpless.

Sally Bones's one eye glittered like the moon. 'Jalal?' she said. 'Jalal the Paw? He's been dead a hundred years! What could you know of Jalal? What do you know?'

'Slow-Time,' gasped Varjak. 'Moving Circles—'

'You?' Sally Bones blinked. Something that might have been fear flashed across her face. 'Is it you?'

Before Varjak could answer, a long, low growl filled the air. Everyone turned to face it.

At the top of the alley, blocking the way out, was a new kind of monster. It was black and bristly, almost as big as a man. Its mouth was full of pointed yellow teeth which dripped with drool. It barked loudly, and took a step towards the cats.

Terror ripped through Sally Bones's gang. Razor, Luger, Wes: they all bolted. They scrambled up the fire escapes and over the walls, away from the monster, away from the alley.

'Come back!' screamed Sally Bones. 'Cowards – we can beat it if we fight together!'

But they weren't listening. Her gang scurried to safety as fast as they could. The thin white cat shook her head with contempt. She stood up reluctantly, letting Varjak go free.

'We'll finish this another time, Varjak Paw,' she said. There was a shimmer of white – and she was gone.

In a single heartbeat, Varjak and Holly were alone with the monster. It looked confused. It barked at the walls, but didn't try to follow the cats up.

'So those Sally Bones stories are true,' breathed Holly. She shook her head. 'I don't know what was going on back there, but I'd swear you had them worried.'

Varjak's head was whirling. Sally Bones knew about Jalal. She knew about the Way, much more than he did. She wasn't even scared of this monster.

'Thanks for keeping quiet about the alleys,' said Holly. 'Come on, let's get out of here, before it gets us,' she urged.

The monster began to lumber towards them. Its

big blunt claws clacked on the pavement as it came. It was incredibly powerful. Even its tail looked as if it could knock them senseless.

Varjak focused. What would Jalal do? Second Skill: Awareness. He looked into its eyes. They were cloudy black. There was pain in those eyes – and there was fear, almost terror, in its scent.

It barked again, a deafening sound. Varjak didn't flinch: he just kept looking into its eyes. If he hadn't once stood before a roaring dog, he would have run away. But compared to those metal monsters, this frightened, barking animal was friendly.

'What are you doing?' hissed Holly. 'Let's go!'

Varjak looked up. He could probably make it over a wall or onto a window ledge, like Sally Bones's gang. He gambled instead and trusted his instincts. This time, he wasn't going to run, he wasn't going to panic. He was going to stand his ground and face it down.

'Don't be afraid,' he said to the monster, in the calmest voice he could manage. It opened its jaws. They were big enough to swallow him whole. 'Don't be afraid,' he whispered.

And then it sprang at him . . .

Slow-Time!
. . . and Holly leaped for cover . . .

Moving Circles!
. . . but Varjak stood his ground . . .

Shadow-Walking?
. . . wrong.

The monster smashed into him. The world turned upside down – and everything went black again.

Chapter Twenty-five

'There are times when it is useful to disappear,' said Jalal.

Varjak was back in Mesopotamia, where the air smelled like cinnamon and tasted of ripe dates. He smiled. It was good to be back. Whatever happened in the real world, there was always Mesopotamia in his dreams.

Jalal stood beside him in the shadow of a wall. And then he was gone.

'Jalal?' said Varjak. His ancestor had disappeared. Even his scent had gone.

'Jalal the Paw, that am I,' said the old cat's voice. But all Varjak could see was a shadow at the base of the wall.

Varjak shook his head. 'That's impossible.'

Jalal appeared again, right next to Varjak. 'Nothing is impossible.'

'Maybe it's possible for you – but I'm not you, Jalal, I can't do these things, I can't go invisible or talk to dogs—'

'Believe something is impossible,' said his ancestor calmly, 'and you will surely fail. But believe in yourself and you can do anything.'

Varjak thought about pigeon hunting with Holly. She believed it was impossible, but he felt sure they could do it if they could just find the right way. Maybe this was the same – and here was Jalal himself offering to show him the Way. Wasn't it worth trying and trying and trying again?

He nodded. 'Teach me, Jalal.'

'Shadow-Walking is the Sixth Skill,' explained the old cat. 'To Shadow-Walk, you must let go of yourself. Like when you stalk your prey and you become your prey – but instead, here you become nothing, nothing at all. You join with the shadow. You become one with the air, and part of the ground. You let go. Try it.'

Varjak slunk towards the wall, willing himself to

disappear. I'm a shadow, he told himself. No one can see me. I'm invisible.

'You are thinking too hard,' said Jalal. 'Shadow-Walking is not done by thinking. Shadows cannot think, after all. Think about nothing. Empty your mind of thoughts.'

Varjak tried to think about nothing; but found himself thinking about thinking about nothing. He tried to empty his mind, but his mind was full of images of emptiness.

'Now you are trying too hard,' said Jalal. 'Perhaps it is too soon. You must know yourself, be sure of yourself, before you can let go of yourself. Do you know who you are?'

Varjak frowned. 'What do you mean?'

'Think about it, Varjak Paw.' Jalal disappeared into the shadow. 'Think hard. For your life depends upon it.'

Chapter Twenty-six

Varjak awoke. He was sprawled on the ground in the alley. His shoulder screamed with pain. Holly was gone.

The bristly, barking monster towered above him, its foul breath in his face. Its big red tongue lolled out, glistening hungrily. It looked like it was getting ready to eat him. He was wrong to trust his instincts; this creature was worse than a dog. It was the most terrifying monster in the world.

He had to do something! Shadow-Walking, the Sixth Skill: *Think about nothing. Empty your mind of thoughts.*

Varjak concentrated. Nothing. Nothing. Nothing.

But it wasn't that easy. The pain in his shoulder filled his mind. He couldn't do it. He couldn't Shadow-Walk.

Varjak looked up desperately at the narrow brick walls of the alley. It felt as if they were closing in on him. If only he could get to the ledge. He tried to stand up, but it hurt too much.

There was no escape now. It was all over. The monster's drooling mouth opened wide . . .

'Cludge,' it said, in a deep, deep voice. Varjak stared, helpless. It blinked those cloudy eyes. Then it licked itself, once. 'Cludge,' it repeated.

Varjak scratched his ears, not quite sure what he was hearing. 'Is that your name?' he said. 'Cludge?'

It panted. A shy smile appeared at the corner of its mouth. 'Cludge,' it affirmed.

Varjak smiled back. Maybe Cludge wasn't going to eat him, after all. 'Varjak,' he said. 'I'm Varjak.'

'Var Jak? Var . . . Varjak. Varjak!'

'That's right, Cludge. I'm Varjak.'

'VARJAK! VARJAK! VARJAK!' barked Cludge.

'You've got it.'

'VARJAK!'

Varjak gingerly shifted his weight onto his front paws. His shoulder twinged, though not as badly as before, and he flopped back onto the ground.

Cludge reached down to lick the wounded shoulder. His big black eyes were cloudy with worry.

'Sorry, Varjak,' he sighed. 'Didn't mean. To hurt.'

'That's OK. I should've run, like the other cats.'

'Cludge was scared. Varjak not scared?'

'No,' he smiled. He was beginning to like this great big creature. Cludge looked fierce, but he seemed gentle inside.

'Cludge alone,' he sniffed. 'Everyone run from Cludge. No friends.'

Varjak looked into Cludge's eyes again. He could see it all in there; he recognized it: his pain, his fear, his loneliness.

'It's all right, Cludge,' he said quietly. 'You're not alone. We'll be friends, you and me.'

'Friends?' panted Cludge. 'Varjak, Cludge, friends?'

Varjak grinned. 'Friends,' he said. He tried to stand up again. This time, his shoulder took the weight.

'Friends!' barked Cludge. He wagged his tail. 'Varjak, Cludge, friends! FRIENDS! FRIENDS!'

'Varjak Paw,' said a gravelly voice, 'this is a first. I've seen a lot of things in this city – I've even seen you hit Razor – but this is truly something else.' Holly jumped down from the wall. 'You did it. You talked to a dog.' She shook her head. 'It's incredible. It's unbelievable. It's—'

'A dog?' said Varjak. Cludge barked.

'Yes, a dog,' said Holly, keeping a safe distance from Cludge. 'What do you *think* it is?'

'But he's not like the other dogs.'

'What other dogs?'

'You know. The metal ones.'

Holly looked baffled. 'I've never seen a dog like that.'

In the distance, a monster shrieked and roared.

'Those ones!' said Varjak. 'The dogs that make that noise!'

Holly shook her head. 'That's not a dog. That's a car.'

'A what?'

'Car!' barked Cludge. 'Cars are fun. Cludge chase cars.'

'So they weren't dogs?' said Varjak.

'Let me get this straight,' said Holly. 'All the time you thought you were talking to dogs, what you were really doing was talking to *cars*?'

Varjak frowned. He was confused. The metal monsters were dogs – he was sure they were! But had anyone else ever called them dogs? No. Now he thought about it, he'd never known for certain what they were. He'd just assumed they were dogs, because they fitted the Elder Paw's description from the tales. They filled his heart with fear; they had foul breath and a deafening sound; and they looked strong enough to kill a man.

But, he had to admit, so did Cludge.

Awareness, the Second Skill: *before you do anything, you must know what you are dealing with. Assume nothing; be sure of the facts.*

That was exactly what he'd failed to do. He'd almost killed himself trying to talk to a car. A beginner's mistake. Not the kind of mistake a cat who knew the Way would make. He wouldn't make it now. And he was sure Sally Bones wouldn't, either.

Holly giggled.

'What's so funny?' Varjak demanded.

She pulled herself together, but only just. 'You,' she said. 'Cars aren't even alive, you moron. You can't talk to a car!'

'You didn't think I could talk to Cludge, either,' reasoned Varjak.

'Cludge only talk to friends,' said the big dog.

'See?' said Varjak. 'Maybe cars only talk to their friends, too.'

Holly couldn't control herself any longer. Her whiskers started to twitch, her body began to shake, and then she cracked up completely. Laughter streamed out of her and flew around the alley like a flock of birds. It was everywhere, it was contagious. Cludge rolled about on the ground, yelping and panting helplessly, and then Varjak found himself laughing too. He couldn't help it; he had to join in with them. It was a good feeling, light and free. He saw it all now, how he'd got it wrong. Of *course* cars weren't dogs: Cludge was a dog!

Cludge was a dog?

Varjak stopped laughing. *Cludge was a dog.* With a dog, he could still save his family from the Gentleman and his cats – if only there was time. 'Cludge, I need your help. I need you to scare a man. Can you do that?'

Cludge stopped yelping and became very serious. He drew himself up to his full height and bared his yellow teeth. Holly's laughter tailed away at the sight. 'Cludge scare everyone,' the great dog said in his deep voice. 'Except Varjak.'

'Then let's go. There's no time to waste.' Varjak turned to Holly. 'Coming?'

'Where?'

'Up the hill. The three of us. We're going to save my family.'

'This is mad,' said Holly. 'But no one messes with Sally Bones and gets away with it – we're not safe in this city any more.' She stood up. 'So all right, Mr Paw, lead the way. Where you go, I go.'

Something in Varjak soared at that moment.

'Thank you,' he said, 'my friends.'

Chapter Twenty-seven

The three friends headed for the hill at top speed. Varjak explained about the Gentleman and his black cats on the way.

He hoped he wasn't too late. With the Elder Paw gone and Father in charge, what would the family do when they faced the Gentleman's cats? What would the Gentleman's cats do to them? Anything could have happened. After all the time he'd been away, the house would surely be different.

Those pictures in his head – the red velvet arm-chair, the china feeding bowls – might not even exist any more.

He was sure of only one thing. They'd have to climb the wall to get in, and Varjak remembered it as the hardest climb of his life.

Thunder growled above the city as they reached the foot of the hill. The sky was violet with the threat of another storm.

'It's up here,' said Varjak, leading the way as lightning flashed overhead.

They climbed the hill as fast as they could. Rain began to fall. It came in stinging whips which lashed into Varjak's nose, his eyes, his ears. He tried to snatch a breath; water filled his mouth, surged down his throat. He choked on it, but kept going, up the hill, one step, two steps, a hundred, a thousand: whatever it took.

The moon stared down at them, a sullen one-eyed sentry in the sky. *Give up*, it seemed to say. *Give up and go away.*

Soaking, straining, panting for breath, they reached the top of the hill as the sky shattered in white light.

What Varjak saw there made his fur prickle. A little stone wall stood before them, half the height of any in the city. It looked old and crumbling, as if it had been neglected for a very long time. Another blast of thunder rocked the earth. Varjak shivered. Could this really be the same wall which enclosed the world he grew up in? The wall that once seemed so high and impossible to climb? Was this the place he had left? Or had everything changed while he was away?

There was a door in the wall. He pushed at it. It wouldn't budge; it was locked. He circled the wall, seeking some familiar sight. A lightning flash revealed the cracks and fissures in the stone where the wild moss grew. At the top of the wall he could see the gnarled upper branches of some stunted, old trees – and there was that single tree which he'd fallen down the night he left home.

Varjak touched its wet bark, and smiled with relief. He recognized it now. Of course it was the same. The place would never change: it was him who had changed.

'This is it!' he shouted happily above the thunder. 'There are trees inside, we can climb down. I'll go first, and . . . Cludge, what's wrong?'

Cludge was shaking. His eyes were cloudy with fear again. 'C-can't climb,' he stammered. 'Cludge can't climb.'

Varjak stared at the huge, powerful dog in disbelief. 'You can't?'

'Of course he can't,' snapped Holly. 'Everyone knows dogs can't climb – we'd be in big trouble if they could. Isn't there another way in?'

'Dogs can't *climb*?'

'No, they can't,' said Holly. She frowned. 'This is the only way in, isn't it? I can tell from your face.'

It felt like falling through the air and never landing. They were so near. But that wall, that old stone wall, stood in the way once again.

'Cludge sorry,' said a small, scared voice beside him. 'Want to help, Varjak.'

Lightning flared up above. Thunder cracked. Rain streamed down Varjak's face like tears. But it was strange; the storm didn't scare him as it had before. Instead, it seemed to enter him from whiskers to tail, filling him with its own wild power, so that he and the storm became one.

There was no turning back now. With or without a dog, he was going to find his family.

'It's all right, Cludge,' he said. 'You wait for us here. Come on, Holly. Let's go inside.'

They left Cludge cowering under the tree. The two cats stormed to the top of the wall. They clambered over the edge and down the other side, through a tangled maze of twisted branches.

Silently, they stole into the garden. They padded over the wet grass and up to the cat door.

'This is it,' whispered Varjak as they slipped through. 'This is the Contessa's house.'

Chapter Twenty-eight

They emerged in the corridor. It was empty. The cat door clicked shut behind them. Holly turned to it at once, nudged it with a paw. It stayed shut.

'Let me try,' said Varjak. He pushed, but it wouldn't open. It had locked from the inside.

'So you can come into this place,' said Holly, 'but you can't leave?'

'The Gentleman must have changed it,' said Varjak, a knot of tension growing in his stomach. This wasn't a good sign.

He looked around the corridor. The thick green windows were closed, the lace curtains drawn. It looked normal – except that, like the garden wall, everything seemed much smaller and older than he remembered. The faded rugs, the stuffy furniture; compared to the city it was more like a display in a shop window than any real place. The silence made it stranger still: there were none of the city sounds here.

There was no one about, either. Not the family, not the Gentleman, not those black cats of his. Yet it smelled strongly of cats, as if there were lots of them very near. His whiskers tingled. This wasn't right. Where were they all?

Varjak and Holly shook the rainwater from their fur and moved stealthily along to the hallway. At the top of the stairs, above the musty carpet, the Contessa's door was closed. Varjak pricked up his ears. He could hear something up there – a long, low, mewling noise – but further down the corridor he thought he could hear cats talking.

'I'll look upstairs,' whispered Holly. 'You check out down here. In case I find them, what do your family look like?'

Varjak paused. 'A bit like me,' he said, 'but different. Be careful. Run if you see a man, or two black cats. They're dangerous.'

Holly headed up the stairs. Varjak edged along the corridor. He tried to empty his mind of thoughts, as Jalal had said, so he could Shadow-Walk. But it was no good. The thoughts kept coming. Where were the family? Were they all right? Would they be glad to see him, or had they forgotten about him already?

He could clearly hear voices now, coming from the front room. The door was half open. He crept up to the edge, where he wouldn't be seen, and peered in.

There they were – the Mesopotamian Blues, alive and well!

Relief flooded through him. He wasn't too late. He hadn't let them down. There was no sign that they'd been hurt. No sign of the Gentleman, or his cats.

It looked like a Family Council was in progress. But it was Julius who sat now on the Contessa's red velvet armchair. The others were clustered around, fiddling with their collars as they listened to him speak. What was going on?

'I don't care,' Julius was saying.

'But things like this don't happen for no reason,' said Father. 'Shouldn't we try to find out what it means?'

'I'm the head of this family now,' said Julius, flexing his muscles. 'Does anyone have a problem with that?'

There were a few mutters around the room, but no one replied. Varjak couldn't believe his eyes. Things really had changed since he'd been away. Julius was acting like a gang boss. It looked like he'd done to Father what Father had done to the Elder Paw.

'If we all agree,' said Julius, 'then the Council is over.'

Varjak took a deep breath, and stepped into the room. They turned to stare at him as if he was a stranger.

'Varjak?' said Mother. 'Is it really you, sweetheart? Look, everyone, he's back!' At once, they cleared a space for him, surrounded him with silver-blue fur and green eyes.

'Varjak Paw! We thought you were lost forever!'

'He's grown, hasn't he?'

'Welcome home, Varjak!'

Home. Finally, he was home. He looked round the family circle. They were purring and beaming at him – Mother, Father and Aunt Juni; Julius and Jasmine; Jay, Jethro and Jerome. They all seemed so glad to see him. It was good to be back.

'Where have you been, son?' said Father.

'Outside.'

'And the Elder Paw?'

Varjak shook his head sadly. 'Gone.'

Julius stepped between Varjak and his parents. 'Things have changed since you disappeared,' he said. 'I'm head of the family now. Father was for a while, but now it's me.'

He stuck his chest out, to underline the point. He was bigger than Varjak remembered him. He'd grown taller; his body had thickened and become more powerful. His collar was tight around his neck. He looked extremely well-fed.

Varjak glanced at Father. He seemed tired and old next to Julius. It was obvious who would win in a fight. Perhaps it had already happened.

'Congratulations,' said Varjak to his big brother.

'That's not all that's changed—' began Father.

'No, things are better for us now than they've ever been,' interrupted Julius. He pressed something down beneath his paw. It was the toy mouse. 'The Gentleman's been very good to us.'

'Him?' said Varjak. 'His cats killed the Elder Paw!'

There was a gasp around the room, but Julius just looked annoyed. 'You're lying,' he said, raking his claws across the mouse. It had become ragged; its fur was wearing away. 'The Gentleman loves us. His cats are our friends. Why would they do a thing like that?'

'They wanted to stop us going Outside—'

'Well, there's your answer,' said Julius. 'They were only trying to help. If you hadn't been doing something wrong . . .'

Varjak bristled. It was Julius who was wrong. Varjak knew he was – but Julius could always make his lies so convincing, and Varjak couldn't find an answer fast enough.

'Now, now,' said Mother. 'Julius is right, Varjak. The Gentleman still feeds us wonderful food every day. As for his cats—' Julius shot her a look, and she

198

coughed. 'Well, that's enough of that,' she said quickly. 'But just look at you, sweetheart. Haven't you grown? And those scars on your face: you've changed so much I hardly recognize you!'

'What scars?' said Varjak – and remembered Ginger, and Razor, and Sally Bones. He smiled. The world Outside had left its mark on him. 'Well, I've had a few fights.'

A voice like milk in the morning purred in his ear. Cousin Jasmine. 'Why Varjak, you're not a little kitten any more!' Varjak's ears perked up. He'd always liked Jasmine more than the others.

'He'll always be our kitten,' said Mother. She licked Varjak's coat, smoothed his fur. He didn't object. He let her warm tongue wash away the rain from the storm and the city's grime, let her strip him of the smell of Outside.

'That's right,' said Julius, glowering at Jasmine. 'He's still a kitten.'

'So what's it like Outside?' said Jay.

'What happened to your collar?' said Jethro.

'And how'd you get those scars?' said Jerome.

'I'll tell you,' said Varjak, though Julius was now glowering at them. 'I'll tell you everything.'

Chapter Twenty-nine

Varjak didn't tell the family about his dreams – he didn't think they'd understand that part – but he told them all about the city: the fights, the friends, the Vanishings. It felt strange to tell his tale at last; it didn't feel real. It was more like a dream or a fantasy. The Mesopotamian Blues, young and old, gazed at him, listening silently, captivated by his descriptions of life Outside the house. By the time he got to Cludge, even Julius seemed enthralled.

'Varjak's brought glory to the family,' said Father when it was over. Varjak did his best to look humble, but it wasn't easy.

'I always said he'd turn out well if we brought him up right,' beamed Mother. Jasmine purred at him. Jay, Jethro and Jerome looked at him with new respect.

But Julius just snorted. 'That's a good tale,' he said, toying with the Gentleman's mouse. 'Except it's only a tale, isn't it? I know you, Varjak Paw. I bet you were so scared you didn't do half those things.' Julius's pupils narrowed. He puffed his fur out, making him look even bigger than he was.

Varjak's throat tightened. A fight was the last thing he wanted at this moment of triumph. He looked into the fireplace. It was cold.

'Yes, sometimes I was scared,' he admitted. 'But everything I said was true.'

'You scrawny little insect,' sneered Julius. 'Who do you think you are, coming back here and lording it up like this? You think we care about your stupid tales?'

'Julius!' cooed Jasmine in her milky voice. 'I do believe you're jealous.'

Julius ignored her. 'He's not even a proper Mesopotamian Blue,' he hissed. 'Never has been, never will be.'

He flicked the toy mouse aside, and stared at Varjak with green eyes full of contempt.

'That's not true, Julius,' said Father. 'Of course Varjak's a Mesopotamian Blue. Only a Blue could do those things.'

'He's not one of us,' growled Julius. 'Eyes the colour of danger. Isn't that right, insect?'

Something rose in Varjak's heart. His mind was catching fire. All those times Julius had made fun of him, made him miserable, made him feel small and weak.

'Don't call me that,' he said.

'Insect,' spat Julius.

'I don't like it. I never liked it.'

'It's what you are. Now come on, I'll squash you flat!'

Something snapped in Varjak. 'ALL RIGHT!' he heard himself yell.

'Don't, Varjak,' said Jasmine. 'He'll kill you—'

Julius hissed at her. She shrank back and was silent like the rest.

Varjak's face was burning. But he had no choice now. He had to go through with it.

Varjak and Julius started to circle each other, stalking around the Contessa's empty armchair. The family made a ring around them. Everyone was watching, silent, with bated breath.

Varjak breathed in–two–three–four, and dropped smoothly into Slow-Time. Julius glared at him with scornful green eyes, and bared his teeth. Varjak glared right back; bared his own teeth. Julius looked surprised.

'Come on, Julius Paw,' said Varjak. 'Squash me flat.'

Julius lunged in.

He was quick for a cat of his size, but Varjak was quicker, more agile, a Moving Circle of pure energy. He stepped aside. Julius bit heavily into space. His teeth cracked together. It sounded painful.

'Don't ever call me an insect again,' said Varjak.

Julius roared. He raked out with a strong, silver-blue paw. Varjak was too fast once more. Julius missed, and lurched into the armchair.

Jay, Jethro and Jerome giggled. Were they laughing at his Moving Circle? Varjak turned, to see them giggling at Julius instead. He smiled, but as he looked away, Julius came at him and cracked the side of his face with vicious strength.

Varjak staggered back. He hadn't expected that. It hurt.

'Insect!' thundered Julius. 'Now you've made me angry!' He launched a flurry of claws. Senses reeling, Varjak dived away just in time. He had to keep breathing, keep the Moving Circle going, or Julius would finish him.

He dodged the furious attacks that followed, becoming a shimmer that Julius couldn't quite hit. The attacks grew wilder, angrier. Varjak stayed a step ahead, just out of reach, as his big brother closed in – until Julius threw everything he had at him in one massive blow. There was no avoiding this one: Varjak had to meet it, head on.

He breathed out–two–three–four. Went deep into his Circle. The power rose within him; and when Julius came, the Circle held true. Varjak turned the blow away, using his brother's own strength against him. Julius went stumbling to the ground.

Varjak grinned. It felt good. Better than the time he'd fought Razor. It was better than anything, a hot, intoxicating glow that pulsed through every fibre of his being. He'd never felt so alive.

Julius was off-balance now, weak and exposed.

Finish him, thought Varjak. Right now. *Let loose the energy.* He'll never fight again.

Do it!

No.

'Enough,' said Varjak Paw. 'Enough, and no more.'

Julius shook his head. 'I'm only just beginning,' he panted. 'Insect.' Julius flung himself through the air, out of control, claws splayed. Varjak leaned away in Slow-Time.

CRASH! Julius smashed head-first into the fire-place. Looked at Varjak with small green eyes, clouded by black ash. Tried to stand up. Couldn't.

It was over.

'Varjak Paw!' cried Jasmine.

'Varjak Paw!' The family hailed his conquest.

'Varjak Paw! Varjak Paw! Varjak Paw!'

He closed his eyes. The victory tasted sweet, like

cinnamon. He'd done it at last. He was a Mesopotamian Blue.

'Varjak Paw! Is that you?'

A gravelly voice! Varjak's heart skipped a beat.

'Holly?'

'Varjak? I'm here!'

Chapter Thirty

It was Holly! Her spiky black-and-white fur burst into the front room. Varjak went to the door to meet her, flushed with victory. But there was a look in her mustard eyes – a look of horror – that wiped the smile off his face the moment he saw it.

'Varjak, it's horrible,' she said. 'We've got to get out of here.' She looked up at the thick green windows, searching for a way out.

'What's horrible?' said Varjak, confused.

'It's the Vanishings . . . this is where they've all gone.' She shuddered. 'The man's not here, and I didn't see those black cats. But there's a room upstairs with a big cage in it, and hundreds of cats in it, only lots of them aren't—' She closed her eyes as if she was trying to block out the memory.

'Aren't what?' he said, afraid of the answer.

'They're not alive.' She looked more shaken than he'd ever seen her in the city.

'Sorry to interrupt you, Varjak,' said Mother, 'but

who is this?' The Mesopotamian Blues were all watching, even Julius, licking his wounds by the fireplace.

'Holly, this is my family,' said Varjak. 'Mother, Father, everyone: meet Holly.'

'Don't worry,' Holly said to them. 'We'll find a way out.'

Father frowned, and turned to Varjak. 'I don't understand,' he said. 'Do you know this cat?'

'This is Holly – my friend from Outside, who I told you about.'

Father looked disgusted. He turned his back on her. They all turned their backs.

'This is not Outside,' said Father. 'Tell this cat to leave us.'

It felt like a slap in the face. Varjak glanced at Holly. She looked as stunned as he felt.

'How could you even think of it?' whispered Mother. 'You should know better than this, sweetheart.'

'Didn't you hear?' protested Varjak. 'She's going to help us get out.'

'But we don't want to get out,' said Mother. 'Where would we go? Who would feed us?'

'Wait a minute,' said Holly. 'Have you seen what's happening upstairs? If you're being fed, it's not for a good reason.'

Father ignored her; he spoke just to Varjak. 'We

haven't been upstairs, because of the black cats. But we know there are other cats up there too.'

'You do?' said Varjak.

'The Gentleman brings them to the house,' said Father. 'He feeds them. Not like he feeds us, not with caviare, but cheap dry food. There are sacks of it in the kitchen. He keeps them alive until – well, we don't know exactly what happens next – but we all agree that the Gentleman would never harm one of us.'

'You're wrong,' said Holly. 'If it's them today, it'll be you tomorrow.'

'We're different,' Father said to Varjak. 'We're special. We're Mesopotamian Blues. As for those common cats,' he shrugged, 'who cares what he does to them? They're nothing.'

'What?' said Holly, ears and whiskers bristling.

'Less than nothing,' said Aunt Juni, as if Holly wasn't there.

'Come on, Varjak, let's go,' said Holly. 'These idiots deserve everything they've got coming.'

Her words made Varjak shiver. He didn't know what to do or say. He looked at Mother.

'We know what we're talking about, sweetheart,' she said, in a gentle, reasonable voice. 'We're not going anywhere.'

His head was spinning. Maybe they were right and Holly was wrong. The Gentleman hadn't harmed them yet; perhaps he never would.

'But what about Holly?' said Varjak.

'She is not one of us,' insisted Father.

Varjak looked at Holly. He looked at his family. There was a twisting, tearing feeling in his guts. He looked at Holly. The family. And Holly again. His insides were being ripped in half. It was impossible.

'We need you here,' said Jasmine.

'You need me?' said Varjak.

Father nodded, very serious. 'Of course we need you, son. You're head of the family now. You can't just leave us.'

'You beat Julius,' said Jay.

'Julius was terrible,' said Jethro.

'But you're the best, Varjak,' said Jerome.

Varjak felt proud inside, proud to be a Blue.

creeeaak

It was the front door, opening.

click CLACK

The Gentleman, entering the house. Two sleek black cats by his shoes.

'Come on,' urged Holly. 'Now!'

She cut towards the corridor. Varjak couldn't move. His mouth felt numb, like ice. He wanted to go with her, but how could he? He finally had what he always wanted: he was a proper Mesopotamian Blue at last!

He couldn't ruin it. He couldn't walk away now.

Holly stopped, on the edge of the front room.
She glanced back at him. He looked away. Shame
pricked his eyes, made him blind. He couldn't meet
her mustard gaze.

'Holly . . .'

'Varjak? What's wrong?'

'I—I can't . . .'

He felt it at once: her invisible barrier, going up,
coming between them. And he knew why. Because
he'd done exactly what she'd always feared her
friends would do. He'd let her down, at the very

moment when she was trying to help. But what else could he do?

'I'm the worst friend in the world,' he whispered.

'Stop,' she said. 'Don't say another word.'

Varjak watched, frozen to the spot, as Holly bolted like she'd been burned, bolted away from him and towards the front door.

The Gentleman's cats were ready for her. In a blur of blackness, moving as one, they blocked her and flung her to the floor.

Varjak's Awareness spun into action, taking in

their smooth, sleek power, their deadly speed. He'd seen everything in the city, even the fearsome Sally Bones, but these black cats were still something else. The way they moved together so perfectly, their identical eyes . . . they were more like machines than anything alive.

They had Holly trapped on the ground. His heart screamed at the sight, but how could he fight them both on his own? They'd destroy him, like they'd destroyed the Elder Paw.

He turned to the family for help, but they turned away. No one could look at him.

The Gentleman closed the front door. He stooped down to touch one of the black cats' collars, and whispered something in its ear.

It left Holly with the other black cat, and marched up to the front room, where it stood blocking the way out. It stared at Varjak and the family with its black eyes. As its gaze fell on him, Varjak's Awareness quickened with a strange, cold sensation.

He took a step towards the black cat. Immediately, it pushed him back. Varjak's hackles rose.

'Don't, son,' said Father. 'You're bringing us into danger.'

'Just let them do what they want,' said Mother, 'and they won't hurt us.'

Varjak's mind was raging. After all they'd been

through together, he'd let Holly down. He'd brought her here. He'd cost her the few moments in which she might have escaped. And now, he couldn't even help her, because that would harm his family, and there was no way he could do that.

He wanted to be a Blue. He was a Blue. He belonged with them. Not her. Them.

He looked on, powerless, as the other black cat dragged Holly up the stairs. She went without a struggle. There was no fight left in her. Varjak watched, silent, unable to move. The last thing he saw was the tip of her tail, vanishing from view. It was like watching his own heart being torn out.

She was gone. The Gentleman went upstairs after her. The black cat who'd been guarding them followed at last, leaving Varjak alone with the family again.

'That's my son,' said Father.

'I knew you'd do the right thing,' said Mother.

'What an ugly little cat she was,' said Cousin Jasmine. Her voice sounded like milk. Sour milk.

Chapter Thirty-one

That evening, Varjak dreamed.

He dreamed he was walking by the Tigris. Date palms swayed in the cinnamon breeze. He looked up at those Mesopotamian stars, no longer so strange. They were part of him now, as he was part of this place. It was peaceful out here. It was home. However hard Jalal's teaching was, it wasn't as difficult as the real world with its decisions and dangers and failures.

Jalal walked beside him. 'The knowledge that was lost is almost restored,' he said. 'There is but one more Skill. This, however, I cannot teach you. I can only tell you its name.'

As he spoke, Varjak wondered what the original Mesopotamian Blue really thought of him. Jalal had never answered that question. Would the old cat be proud that Varjak had stood by his family? He'd faced a terrible choice, and he had chosen the Mesopotamian Blues. It hurt inside when he thought of Holly; so he tried not to, and looked at his silver-blue ancestor instead.

'What is the Seventh Skill, Jalal?'

'The Seventh Skill is to Trust Yourself. There. Your training is now complete. Keep the Way alive, Varjak Paw.'

Jalal glided down to the water's edge.

'Wait!' called Varjak. 'I don't understand. Show me what it means.'

'Trusting Yourself is a Skill, like Open Mind,' said Jalal. 'But where the First Skill looks outwards, the Seventh looks inwards. This is the hardest Skill of all. For someone who thinks he is not worthy even to be himself, it could be impossible.'

Varjak hung his head, tried to look away from Jalal's amber gaze. But there was no avoiding his ancestor's words. They seemed to reach right into his heart.

'What have I taught you, my son? A cat must be free, must be true: true to itself. When you said you were not worthy to be a Mesopotamian Blue, I knew not whether to laugh or cry. You see, who you are and where you come from count for nothing with me. The only thing that counts is what you do.'

Varjak gasped at his ancestor. He couldn't believe what he was hearing.

'Aren't we the noblest of cats?' he said.

'We are whatever we choose to be,' said Jalal. 'If being a Blue means anything, it means following my Way. Any cat who does that is one of mine. All you need do is Trust Yourself, and I say you are worthy to be a Blue.' He smiled. 'What say you now, Varjak Paw?'

'But my eyes . . .'

'What colour are your eyes?'

'They're the wrong colour. The colour of danger.'

'Which is?'

Varjak hesitated. 'I don't know,' he admitted. 'I've never seen them.'

'Come and join me, my son.'

Varjak glided down to the water's edge.

'Look at me,' said Jalal. 'Am I worthy to be a Mesopotamian Blue?'

'Of course you are!'

'Now look into the river,' said Jalal. 'What do you see?'

Varjak peered at the still
surface of the Tigris. He saw
the stars shimmering deep
inside. Saw the moon rising
in the east.

And saw two silver-blue
cats with amber eyes, calmly
looking back at him.

Chapter Thirty-two

Varjak awoke from his dream in the front room. It was still dark Outside as he looked around. The family were gathered round him in a circle, by the Contessa's empty armchair.

His mind was like the sky after a storm. Everything was clear and sharp. He knew what he had to do.

With one leap, he sprang onto the red velvet armchair. No one tried to stop him; not Father, not Julius. It was his. The power was his, and only he could decide what to do with it.

'Now,' he said, 'I need the truth. Has anyone seen the Contessa since the Gentleman came to the house?' They shook their heads. 'So unless we do something ourselves, we're at his mercy. How often is he here?'

'He goes out a lot,' said Father.

'And the black cats? Do they go with him?'

'Varjak, you're head of the family,' said Julius. 'I'm not disputing that. But why do you ask these questions? It's only going to cause trouble. Why can't you just accept things as they are?'

'Because something's happening up there, something bad. I'm going to find out what it is. I'm going to get my friend back. And if I have to, I'm going to fight those black cats to do it.'

'Whatever's going on up there,' said Mother, 'it doesn't affect us, sweetheart. We're different.'

Varjak shook his head. 'We're not different. We're not special. We're cats, just the same as the others.' They looked at him as if he'd gone mad. 'Didn't you hear what Holly said? She's right. Maybe not today, maybe not tomorrow, but one day soon, the Gentleman's coming for us too. His cats killed the Elder Paw to stop us leaving. He's got something planned for us. I know he has.'

A murmur went round. They were thinking about it. But they weren't convinced yet.

'Even if you're right,' said Father, 'how can we fight those black cats? They're too strong.'

'The Elder Paw fought them,' said Varjak. 'They beat him, but he gave them a fight first, a good fight. If we work together, we can do it. That's what I believe. Who's coming with me?'

He looked around the family circle.

Mother, Father and Aunt Juni looked away. Julius and Jasmine looked away. Jay, Jethro and Jerome looked away.

Varjak Paw was on his own again.

'All right,' he said. 'If you change your minds, you know where to find me.'

He came down off the chair and marched out of the circle, out of the room, into the corridor. No one came with him. He didn't expect them to. It was all right. Like being in the city again, he had nothing to rely on but himself, and the Skills Jalal had taught him. Nothing else.

He slunk to the foot of the stairs. Holly was up there somewhere. And so were the Gentleman's cats. How was he going to get past them? He'd need to be invisible. He was going to have to Shadow-Walk: the only Skill he couldn't master.

He took a deep breath. This time, it had to work. There was no other way.

He remembered his dreams. *You must know your-self, be sure of yourself, before you can let go of yourself. Do you know who you are?*

Yes, I do, he thought. I'm Varjak Paw. Nothing less and nothing more.

He relaxed, let go, and merged with the shadows at the foot of the stairs. The world flickered faintly around him.

One of the Gentleman's cats came out of the Contessa's room. It stood at the top of the stairs, sur-veying the scene with its black eyes. Would it see him? It turned his way for a moment – but looked right through him.

Varjak placed a paw on the first step. The black cat didn't react. It was as if he didn't exist.

Slyly, slowly, slithering low, Varjak Shadow-Walked the stairs. The Gentleman's cat just sat there, unaware. It couldn't see him. No one could. He was invisible; he could go anywhere. But where was he going? What was he going to see? He remembered Holly's face as she came into the front room. Whatever it was that lay ahead, it wasn't good.

At the top of the stairs, he heard mewling. It made his fur prickle: it was the sound of fear. But he had to face it. However awful, he had to learn the truth about the Gentleman, the Vanishings and the Contessa's room. That was the only way he could save Holly.

His Awareness tingling with danger, Varjak crept past the Gentleman's cat and up to the room. Sticking to the shadows so he couldn't be seen, he looked in.

It was just as Holly had said. There was a cage in there. It had a solid metal door and sharp wire mesh. It was full of cats, street cats with no collars. But they weren't tough or menacing. The air was thick with the scent of their fright. Varjak could taste it, bitter on his tongue. They were cowering from the Gentleman as he reached into the cage; cowering from the black cat that prowled by his shoes.

Varjak craned his head right back, and saw the Gentleman pluck out a tortoiseshell cat from the cage. She was mewling pitifully; so were the cats around her.

The Gentleman closed the cage door and locked it up with a lever. Varjak had to hold himself still as the shiny black shoes clicked past, a whisker away. The Gentleman was carrying the tortoiseshell out of the room, dangling her by the scruff of the neck. The black cat stayed behind, standing guard over the others.

It took all Varjak's control to remain there in the shadows. The urge to flee clawed at his chest. The cage, the cats, the smell: it was like a nightmare. But he had to trust himself, be true to himself. Downstairs he had known that it was right to come up here. And it was still right. There could be nothing worse for a free cat than to be locked up in a cage like this. Even if it never affected the Blues, this was more important than family, more important than anything. He had to find a way to release Holly and the others.

But where was she? He looked into the cage again – and finally glimpsed her in a corner. Holly was all right! Varjak could see that she was talking to someone. A thin, frightened-looking, chocolate-brown cat. Was it possible? Varjak looked closer. His heart skipped a beat.

It was Tam! There she was: scared, but still alive after all this time!

So Holly was right about the Vanishings. This was where they ended up. But why?

'Where's he taking that tortoiseshell?' Holly was asking Tam. 'What's he going to do with her?'

Tam shook her head. 'We don't know. But that's the end of her. Once he picks you, it's over.' She shuddered.

'It doesn't take long,' said another cat.

In the shadows, Varjak's scalp prickled. What didn't take long? What was going on here? And why was his mouth so dry?

'Can't we get out of this cage?' he heard Holly ask.

'Think we haven't tried?' said Tam. 'It only opens from outside. And even if you could open it – how are you going to get past *them*? Those black cats are the ones who got us in the first place.'

Varjak felt cold. It was that strange sensation again: being watched by something not quite alive, not quite dead. He'd felt it downstairs when he met a black cat's eyes. What did it mean? It couldn't be coming from the black cat this time, because it wasn't looking at him.

Throat tightening, only just holding back the fear, Varjak followed his Awareness. And now he saw where the sensation came from. It wasn't one gaze he felt, but many.

There were other cats in the room, heaped up in a box. They didn't move; didn't talk; didn't breathe. He looked into their eyes. They were wide open, but they didn't blink. They weren't eyes at all. They were shiny, coloured glass, with a black slash through the middle.

Varjak's head began to spin. What was it Holly had said? 'They're not alive.' No. They were just like the toys in the city – but turned off.

The Gentleman came back into the room. He

was carrying the tortoiseshell cat. But it wasn't quite the same any more. It had become totally still. It didn't move. Didn't breathe. Didn't blink its glassy eyes.

It had a new collar, tight around its neck. The Gentleman touched the collar. And as it opened its mouth to speak, Varjak knew with awful, sickening certainty what words it would say.

'I am very well thank you please,' said the tortoise-shell in a hollow little voice.

Its smiling head nodded up and down, up and down, until the Gentleman touched its collar again and it was still once more.

It was a toy cat now, like the others: a perfect, preserved, furry toy that seemed almost alive, because it once was. So were the rest of them, every last one. Not quite alive. Not quite dead. Not cats any more, but toys.

Varjak wanted to scream. This was wrong. He'd never seen anything so wrong.

The Gentleman placed the tortoiseshell carefully in the box, and riffled through it, counting up his toys. Varjak turned his eyes away from the sight. And the cats in the cage began to howl.

Chapter Thirty-three

The Gentleman's shoes clicked past Varjak as he flicked off the light, and headed downstairs. The black cat went with him.

Fury. Pure, white-hot fury seared through Varjak's body, surged through his muscles, scorched away his fear. There was nothing in his mind but what the Gentleman had done to these cats. It had to be stopped, now, while he still had the advantage of surprise. There was not a second to waste.

He came out of the shadows into the Contessa's room. The howling stopped at once. Everyone in the cage looked at him. A hundred cats' eyes, glowing in the dark. How to set them free?

He'd seen the Gentleman pull a lever to lock the cage. There it was, halfway up. One more climb for Varjak Paw.

The wire mesh cut into his pads as he scrambled up, but at least it had grips, more than the garden wall. Varjak hooked both paws round the lever. He

pulled down with all his weight – and the lever
clicked.

The metal door swung open. Cats began to
stream out. They were pushing and shoving, fighting
each other to get away first.

'Wait!' cried Varjak. 'Everyone! We have to work
together—'

No one was listening. They were running in a panic out of the darkness of the Contessa's room. Varjak leaped down off the cage. It was chaos on the ground. Paws and claws and tails like snakes writhed as a hundred cats fought for their freedom.

This wasn't going according to plan. Where were Tam and Holly? They could help him, if Holly would forgive him.

A howl of pain came from somewhere outside the room. Varjak clambered over the paws and claws, out of the door, onto the landing, into the light.

The black cats were at the top of the stairs. Both of them.

Together, they were terrifying. No one could get past them. Strewn beside them were the bodies of those from the cage who'd made it out first. They'd been swatted aside mercilessly, and were either out cold or dead; Varjak couldn't tell. The others were trying desperately to get back into the Contessa's room, where they thought they'd be safe.

It was carnage. But in the middle of it all, Varjak felt strangely calm. There was no way back for him. This wasn't going to be like fighting Julius, or even Razor. This was something else. It was life, or death. That simple.

Like a dancer, he picked his way through the chaos of cats. They made space for him. A profound silence settled on the top of the stairs.

Varjak looked at the two black cats, and started to breathe deeply, filling his lungs. He was getting stronger and better every time. The power was growing within him, like a living thing, and he could feel it again, rising up now. This was what he was born to do. This was it. This was the moment he'd been waiting for all his life.

Fourth Skill: Slow-Time. He sucked in the air, slowed himself down.

Fifth Skill: Moving Circles. Varjak came at the Gentleman's cats, powerful as a pulsing breath.

Sixth Skill: Shadow-Walking. Varjak flickered out of sight. The black cats' whiskers twitched, as if they knew something was about to happen, but they didn't know what.

Varjak's Moving Circle lifted him up, flying, an arc of vengeance aimed at the enemy. For the Elder Paw. For Holly and Tam. For every cat who'd Vanished off the streets.

The power rose in Varjak's paws. Claws slid out, white knives of fury, and slashed! slashed! slashed! the Gentleman's cats.

Varjak was out of the shadows now. All the energy, all the darkness and light was flowing through him, going out in blow after blow after blow. Everyone who'd ever put him down, every time he'd walked away: all his anger and his pain went into that attack.

It felt overwhelming, a massive rush of power, almost more than he could control. He could win this fight. He could beat anyone, because he knew the Skills; he kept the Way alive. Inside him, everything Jalal had passed on was coming together. And around him, he could hear the street cats, no longer mewling in fear, but cheering as he lashed into their enemy. It couldn't be long before they joined in; and then the battle would be theirs.

He had one of the black cats backed against the wall. Varjak looked into its eyes. Even now, they showed no expression.

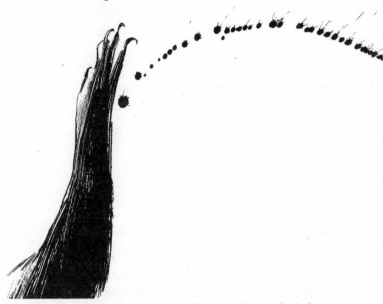

He launched another Circle, ripped right across its face. It didn't blink. No blood came out of the wound. Varjak was tearing it apart, but it didn't bleed. How could that be? He hit it with his best shots, shots he knew should knock out any normal cat – but it stayed standing. It didn't go down. And now he'd lost the element of surprise.

The black cat hit back. It was incredibly fast, even with Varjak in Slow-Time. He arced aside, and only just dodged.

The two black cats glanced at each other. And then they came for him, as they'd come for the Elder Paw in the garden, long ago.

Two bodies moving perfectly, one on each side. Varjak spun a Circle as wide as he could imagine. Moving quick as thought, he deflected one blow, then another, then another, turning them away.

The Circle held. He could feel the energy crackling through him. But the black cats kept coming, relentless, tireless, perfect. Two of them. They didn't give him a moment to think. Never an opening, never a chance. It took all his power, all his concentration, to fend them off. And slowly, they forced him back, back, back towards the Contessa's room.

SMASH!

One of the black cats broke through his Circle. His defences were down. He reeled, off balance. It leaped on him, wrestled him to the ground.

Varjak twisted away, but it was no good. His enemy had him now. It was beating him into the floor.

Hard to breathe. Where were the others? Why weren't they helping? Must break free. Varjak lashed out.

The weight pressed down on him, pinning his paws, crushing his lungs. Varjak gagged. No air. Black eyes filled his sight.

He'd used all the Skills, and they weren't enough. The Way wasn't enough.

But there had to be a way to win. There had to.

At the edge of his vision, he saw a flash of black-and-white fur. A gravelly voice. 'The collars!'

The collars? Varjak looked at the black cat's neck. It wore a collar like the toy cats. He looked into its eyes. So strange. Not like cats' eyes. Glassy.

Glass. There were glass. Like the toys.

Not quite alive; not quite dead. If the Gentleman could make a toy cat, why not a fighting cat? A perfect machine: couldn't be killed, didn't bleed, never gave up. Could be turned on or off . . . from the collar.

Last chance.

He sucked in the air, sucked it all in, and let it out

in one last blast, a desperate lunge for the throat. His teeth closed around the collar. Wrenched back. And ripped right through it.

The collar curled off the black cat's neck. Its eyes opened wide in surprise. It started to raise a paw, but it was slowing, slowing. And slowly, almost gracefully,

it
ground
down
to
a
stop.

Chapter Thirty-four

There was silence at the top of the stairs. The Gentleman's cat was finished. Its body lay stiff and crumpled on the floor. It wasn't terrifying any more. It looked like what it was: a broken toy.

Varjak stood up, shaking, exhausted. He couldn't believe he'd done it. With all his Skills, he was no match for the black cats. He'd fought the fight of his life, yet the truth was, they were better than real cats in almost every way. But they could never be alive like a real cat. That was their strength; it was also their weakness. Somehow, he'd made it count.

The other black cat was staring at the broken toy, as if it couldn't believe what had happened either. It nudged the crumpled body. There was no response. No movement. No life.

It stood up, very slowly, and came towards Varjak. He knew what was coming. This one would never let him near its collar. It was going to avenge its twin. It was going to destroy him. And for all the world, he couldn't think how to stand against it.

But it stopped just before it reached him, and looked him in the eyes. For the first time, Varjak thought he saw a flicker of expression there. It looked sad, terribly, terribly sad.

It wasn't fighting any more. No, it was holding its neck out. It could beat him, it could beat anyone, but it was holding its neck out, as if it wanted him to cut its collar too.

Varjak hesitated. After all this time, fearing and hating the black cats, he'd never thought they might have feelings of their own. But the two of them had always been like one; and now, without its other half, even the perfect fighting machine was useless.

Varjak thought he understood. He leaned towards the black cat. It didn't move away, didn't resist. Very gently, he cut its collar. Its eyes widened for an instant –

– and then it, too, ground down to a stop.

It was over.

'He's done it!'

'He's beaten them!'

Everyone was shouting now.

'We're *free*!'

Where was Holly? At that moment, she was all he could think of. Where was she? She'd figured out how to stop the cats. She was the one who'd done it.

'Kind of sad, those black cats,' said a gravelly voice behind him. 'One couldn't work without the other.'

Varjak turned to face her, his heart aching. Would she forgive him?

'Holly, I'm sorry. I should've come with you—'

Her mustard eyes were smiling. 'I know. But you made up for it. Because you're not the worst friend in the world, Mr Paw. Not by a long shot.'

They grinned at each other.

'Varjak – you did it!' said Tam. She was breathless and her eyes were shining. 'I told her you'd do it. Didn't I tell you, Holly?'

'Tam,' he said, 'it's good to see you again!'

Cheers were going up. Some of the cats from the cage were starting to head downstairs.

'Wait!' shouted Holly. Her gravelly voice stilled them instantly. 'It's not over yet,' she warned. 'We have to find a way out. The house is all locked, all the windows, all the doors. So we've got to find another way. We're going down, but quietly. No one does anything unless we tell you to. We're not bossing you around; we just know what's going on here. Understand?'

There was a ripple of agreement. Varjak marvelled at the way she took control. He smiled to himself as they led the cats down the stairs, in a stealthy, silent column. He had his friends back, both of them. They'd beaten the black cats. They'd done the impossible.

After all he'd been through, maybe, just maybe, everything was going to come good at last.

'Varjak! Varjak! Help!'

He looked down. It was Julius, howling.

Julius, in the Gentleman's grip.

The Gentleman, waiting for them at the foot of the stairs.

The column of cats froze in fear. Varjak could see his family on the edge of the front room, trembling, powerless. They were all powerless before the Gentleman. The black cats were gone, but they were nothing compared to the man who made them.

click CLACK

The Gentleman dropped Julius and stepped towards the stairs, shouting in a voice like thunder. The column of cats cracked and began to break.

'Wait!' cried Holly, but no one was listening now.

245

The street cats panicked, turned tail, fled upstairs. Julius scurried back to his family. In the space of a heartbeat, Varjak, Holly and Tam stood alone as the Gentleman came for them.

His shadow stretched out before him. It covered the stairs, draping them in darkness even before he reached them. His shoes shone like black ice. As they clicked closer, step by step, Varjak could see his own reflection, looming larger in their blackness.

How could he let himself believe that everything would work out? He should have known better. He hated himself for having that moment of hope, because now the hope was gone, there was nothing left at all.

'There's no way out, is there, Varjak?' said Tam.

'No.'

'Looks like goodbye,' said Holly. 'We go down fighting?'

'We go down fighting,' said Varjak Paw.

The Gentleman's waxy white hand reached out for him. Huge enough to hold his whole body. Strong enough to break his neck.

Varjak bared his teeth. Ready to bite. To fight to the death. And it *would* be death. How else could it end?

The hand closed around his neck, and –

CRASH! The smash of breaking glass. A roar like the sky ripping open: 'LEAVE MY FRIENDS ALONE!'

– and the hand let go. Varjak looked up to see the biggest, blackest monster in the world.

Cludge, it was Cludge! The great dog had come through! He'd shattered the windows of the Contessa's house!

Cludge was ferocious. Even Varjak shook at the sight of him.

Cludge roared. The Gentleman cowered. He backed away from the stairs, hands in the air, shaking with terror.

It was something Varjak never expected to see. This almighty man, so vast, so powerful; he'd made the toy cats, the black cats. He was responsible for the Vanishings. He could do anything. And yet even he, with all his power, had something he was scared of, something he couldn't face. And faced with Cludge, the Gentleman became like a little boy, lost and frightened and all alone.

Cludge circled around him, growling and snarling and snapping his teeth. He forced the

Gentleman over to the broken green window, and then he came at him with big blunt claws.

The Gentleman screamed. He turned and ran, out of the window, out of the house. With a wink at the cats, Cludge leaped after him – and chased him screaming into the night.

Chapter Thirty-five

The Gentleman was gone. A great cheer went up. The cats from the cage came charging downstairs.

Varjak Paw slumped to the floor. He should have felt like cheering too, but he didn't. All he wanted was a quiet place to rest.

Some chance.

'Varjak Paw! You did it!' said Julius.

'Varjak and his friends!' They were swamped by admiring green eyes. The Mesopotamian Blues swept them up and carried them on their shoulders. Around them, the street cats were taking over the Contessa's house. They were everywhere, celebrating their release, enjoying their freedom.

'Thank Jalal that's over,' said Mother, above the racket. 'Now how are we going to get back to normal?'

'Good thing there's all that dry food,' said Father. 'It's not caviare, but it'll do.'

Varjak stared at them, shocked. 'You don't want

to stay here, after everything that's happened?'

'We can't go Outside,' said Father.

'This is our home,' said Jasmine, 'the Contessa's house.'

'But there's no Contessa any more,' said Varjak. 'No more Gentleman. It's just us. We're on our own in the world.' He heard a snuffling noise. It was Jay, Jethro and Jerome. 'Don't be scared,' he said. 'We'll start again. We'll find a new home somewhere. Just like Jalal, when he left Mesopotamia. Except this time it'll be ours, because we'll make it ourselves.'

'Var! Jak! Paw!'

'Cludge!' The family scurried aside as the colossal dog leaped back through the window. Tam turned to Holly, her eyes wide open with wonder.

'I don't believe it,' she whispered. 'He actually talked to a dog? A real, proper dog?'

'He's called Cludge,' said Holly. 'He's a friend.'

Cludge's tail wagged merrily. That cloudy look was completely gone from his eyes. They were the clearest black now, and they sparkled with a new life. 'Man gone now,' he panted. 'Won't come back.'

Varjak grinned. 'You saved us all, Cludge. But how did you climb the wall?'

Cludge drew himself up to his full height. 'Wall scare Cludge. But friends need Cludge.' He shrugged. 'So Cludge climb wall.'

More cheers were going up. Some of the cats

from the cage had found the Gentleman's caviare. They were feasting like they'd never feasted before. Others were streaming through the shattered green window, returning to their lives Outside, as the sun began to rise after the long, dark night.

Varjak turned to his family. 'That's where I'm going,' he said. 'That's where I belong.'

'But – you and your friends, you saved us,' said Julius. 'You're head of the family. You can't go now.'

Varjak smiled at his brother. 'I think maybe it's time there wasn't a head of the family any more,' he said. 'There must be a better way of doing things.'

'Show us, Varjak,' said Jasmine.

'I'll show you how to hunt, to fight, to live Outside – if you come with me.'

He looked around the family circle. One by one, they all looked down. But he didn't feel alone. He felt free.

'Varjak, thank you for saving us,' said Father. 'You were right about the Gentleman; we were wrong about your friends. We were wrong about a lot of things. But we can't come Outside with you. Not yet, anyway.'

'If you ever need us,' said Mother, 'we'll be here.'

'I understand,' said Varjak. And at that moment, for perhaps the first time in his life, he really did.

They said their farewells, and then Varjak turned to Holly and Tam.

'So, do you want to be in a gang, then?' he said. Tam nodded and grinned.

'There's only one gang I want to be in,' said Holly, 'and that's ours.'

'Cludge too!' barked the big dog.

Cludge carried them out. As they went, the friends talked and laughed together about the things they had done and the things they would do. Many of the cats they'd freed from the cage followed them, like they were the leaders of a gang.

So much lay ahead of them. Anything was possible now.

It was a beautiful morning. The earth was decked out in dewdrops. The open air was fresh and clean. And up in the clear blue sky, the sun was rising with the promise of a new day, dawning on the wide world, shining bright and amber, like the eyes of Varjak Paw.

OUT NOW:

THE OUTLAW VARJAK PAW